Mary-Kate and Ashley

Sweet 16

Win a
$500
shopping spree!
Details on page 131.

Mary-Kate and Ashley
Sweet 16

Suddenly Sisters

By Emma Harrison

HarperEntertainment
An Imprint of HarperCollins*Publishers*

A PARACHUTE PRESS BOOK

A PARACHUTE PRESS BOOK

Parachute Publishing, L.L.C.
156 Fifth Avenue, Suite 302
New York, NY 10010

Published by
♣HarperEntertainment
An Imprint of HarperCollins*Publishers*
10 East 53rd Street, New York, NY 10022-5299

ISBN 0-06-059615-5

HarperCollins®, ♣®, and HarperEntertainment™ are trademarks of HarperCollins
Publishers Inc.

First printing: March 2005

Printed in the United States of America

10 9 8 7 6 5 4 3 2 1

chapter one

"I can't believe we're still talking about this," I said over my shoulder to my sister, Ashley. "I've apologized about a million times."

We were standing in line in the cafeteria at school, waiting to pay for our lunches. For the fifth time that day she had brought up the dress I'd borrowed for my date with Liam the weekend before. Well, borrowed and then ruined by spilling ketchup all over it. But it wasn't my fault! That restaurant should not have waiters on roller skates! A new trainee smashed right into me as I was coating my fries. It wasn't as if I'd ruined the dress on purpose.

"I just wish you'd told me you were going to Rockin' Robin's," Ashley replied, digging through her bag for her wallet. "I mean, no one wears good

1

clothes to that place. Every time we go there, someone comes out looking like the loser of a food fight."

She paid for our lunch, and I led the way through the cafeteria toward our usual table. Melanie Han, Brittany Bowen, and Lauren Glazer were already sitting there, chatting as they flipped through the script for the spring play. Lauren was the assistant director, and Melanie had just found out that morning she was chosen to be the costume designer. She had been poring over the script between classes all day.

"Okay, say I *had* told you where we were going," I said, raising my shoulders slightly as I gripped my tray with both hands. "Would you really have said no?"

Ashley paused and looked at me. I knew I had her. Neither one of us ever said no when the other one wanted to borrow something.

"Okay, no. I wouldn't have said no," Ashley said finally, rolling her eyes. She flipped her long blond hair over her shoulders as she sat down. "But you still should have warned me. It's just . . . common courtesy."

"Alright, alright," I said, dropping into the chair next to Melanie's and placing my messenger bag on the empty seat beside me. "I swear it'll never happen again."

"Thank you," Ashley replied with a smile.

"I can't believe it," Melanie said with a gleam in her dark eyes. She put the script away and turned her attention to us. "You guys are *still* talking about that dress?"

"Not anymore, I hope," I told her, grabbing my bottle of iced tea and shaking it up.

"Sheesh! At least it's only one dress, Ash," Brittany said as she took a bite of her pasta. "I can't even tell you how many of my outfits have hit the Dumpster since my brother, Lucas, was born."

"What do you mean?" Lauren asked.

"The kid's a walking disaster," Brittany said. "I mean, when he's not spitting up on you, he's throwing his food or knocking stuff over. And don't even get me started on the diapers."

"Oh! But he's so cute!" I said, thinking of baby Lucas's pudgy little cheeks and his dimpled arms and legs. He was always laughing and gurgling, and he *loved* to be tickled. I knew from firsthand experience.

"Yeah, cute like a mini-monster," Brittany joked, causing Melanie to snort a laugh. "I'm only kidding. I love the little guy, but my life has been insane since he came along."

"Well, when there's a baby around, you have to expect that kind of thing," Lauren said with a shrug.

"Exactly. Mary-Kate and her ketchup disaster were *un*expected," Ashley added.

"Alright! That's it! I'm never touching your stuff again, and you're never touching mine!" I said with a laugh. "It's been decided!"

"Please! You guys, at least you *have* someone to borrow stuff from. You should appreciate it," Melanie said. "It stinks being an only child."

Ashley and I exchanged a look. Melanie's father was a fashion designer—that was where she got her eye for costumes—and all his friends were fashion designers, too. Her closet was constantly filled to bursting, and she hardly ever wore the same outfit twice.

"Why would you need to borrow stuff?" Lauren asked as she worked a little braid into her long brown hair. "Your dad brings home an entire new wardrobe for you every season."

"Yeah, Mel. You have the life," Ashley added.

"And I don't care what you say, Brittany," I put in. "I'd love to have a little baby brother or sister to play with."

As I dug into my lunch, I saw Brittany and Melanie exchanging a mischievous look.

"What?" Ashley asked, noticing their expressions as well.

"I was just thinking," Brittany said, folding her arms on the table. "If you guys think our lives are so great, why don't you come stay with us for a little while and see for yourselves?"

"Ooh . . . interesting," Lauren said, her blue eyes gleaming as she dropped the braid. "An experiment."

"Yeah. Ashley can stay with me and see if I really have 'the life,'" Melanie said, scrunching her fingers to make air quotes. "And Mary-Kate can stay with Brittany and the adorable baby."

"For how long?" Ashley asked, leaning forward excitedly. Clearly she liked the idea.

"I don't know," Brittany said. "A week?"

I looked at Ashley across the table, and we both smiled slowly. Sleepovers were one thing, but an entire week living in a different house, finding out what our friends' lives were really like? This could be totally cool!

"Sounds like fun," I said finally.

"Yeah," Ashley added with a nod. "We're in."

Now all we had to do was get Mom and Dad to approve.

"Thank you, Mr. Han," my mother said into her cell phone while Mary-Kate and I stood by, listening in. "Okay . . . Paul. Yes. And thanks for taking the time to speak with me."

She hung up the phone and turned around to smile at us.

"Well?" I asked, feeling about to burst from all the excitement.

"He said yes," Mom replied, placing the phone on the kitchen counter. "Looks like we're losing Ashley for a week."

I squealed giddily. A whole week living in Melanie's palace of a house with her fashion-designer dad! And next week was Fashion Week, when all the big designers showed their new collections in a major fashion show on the beach. I bet there were going to be supermodels and press people all over the place. This was going to rock!

"We're losing Mary-Kate, too," our dad said, coming in from his office, where he had been on the phone with Brittany's mom. "The Bowens said yes as well."

"Cool!" Mary-Kate said. "I can't wait!"

Mom and Dad looked at each other and our mother sighed. Dad walked over to her and put an arm around her shoulders. Suddenly they looked majorly depressed. I hoped they weren't having second thoughts.

"You guys?" I said, my brow wrinkling. "Is everything okay?"

"Sure. It's just . . . you girls are really growing up," Mom said.

"Mom!" Mary-Kate said, wrapping her arms around our mother's waist. My mother ran a hand over Mary-Kate's recently dyed brown, wavy hair, and Mary-Kate grinned at her. "It's just a week! It's no big deal!"

"Besides, it'll be good practice for when the girls go off to college," Dad said, tousling my hair as well. "Like a test run."

"See?" I said, resting my head against Dad's shoulder. "It's going to be a learning experience, for all of us."

Mom laughed, kissed the top of Mary-Kate's head, then pulled me to her and did the same to me.

"Alright, you two," she said. "Go do your homework."

"Mom!" Mary-Kate and I both semi-whined.

"What?" she said with a smirk. "I have to lay down the law while I still can."

I shook my head and laughed.

Mary-Kate trudged up the stairs behind me as we headed back to our rooms. Her steps might have been heavy, but even the thought of writing a ten-page history paper couldn't bring me down right then. I was going to spend the next week living in the biggest house in town, rubbing elbows with fashionistas.

Practice for college? Maybe for my parents. But if this was what college was going to be like, they could sign me up right now!

"Whatcha doing?" Ashley asked, practically skipping into my room on Sunday evening.

"Uh . . . packing," I said, dropping my favorite graphic tee into my duffel bag. "Shouldn't you be doing the same thing?"

"I'm done," Ashley replied. "Oh, maybe you shouldn't bring that top," she added, glancing into my bag.

"Why?" I asked.

"It's your favorite, isn't it?" she asked. "You remember what Brittany said about the baby ruining all her clothes . . . ?"

"Good point," I said, biting my bottom lip. "But if I only bring my cruddier clothes, then what am I supposed to wear to school?"

"Another good point," Ashley said, considering. "Maybe you should bring two sets of stuff—one for school and one for Lucas duty."

"Wow. We are just full of good points today," I said with a grin. I dropped to the floor and pulled another bag out from under my bed so I could fill it up with sweats and old tanks and T-shirts. "I can't believe I have to pack two bags for one week."

"Hey, I packed three," Ashley said, perching on the edge of my desk chair.

"Three?" I echoed, raising my eyebrows.

"What? I'm going to be hanging with the A-list. Who knows how many outfits I'll need?" Ashley replied, her blue eyes wide.

I cracked up laughing and shook my head at her. *Be prepared* wasn't just the Boy Scouts' motto. It was Ashley's motto as well. I opened the third drawer of my dresser, pulled out a bunch of clothes normally reserved for working out, and dumped them into my second bag.

"That should do it," I said, zipping both bags shut. "I'm so psyched to play with the baby."

"And I'm so psyched to play with all the clothes," Ashley responded. "I don't know what Melanie was thinking. Her life is so exciting."

"Yeah, and having a baby around must be so much fun," I said. "Brittany had to be messing with us."

"Well, I guess we're gonna find out," Ashley said, standing.

"Girls! Let's go! Your father and I will be waiting outside!" Mom yelled up the stairs.

"So . . . good luck!" I said to Ashley, giving her a huge bear hug.

"You, too! I'm gonna miss you," she replied.

"I'm gonna miss you, too," I said.

I pulled my duffel bags onto my shoulders and grinned at her before heading downstairs.

Even though I would be seeing Ashley in school every day, I really was going to miss her. Ashley and I had never lived apart in our lives. It would be weird not chatting in her room before bed like we always did, or checking out each other's outfits every morning. But I knew that in a week we would be back under the same roof. For now it was time to start my brand-new life. I couldn't wait to see what would happen next!

chapter two

"So, Ashley, do you want to stay in one of the guest rooms or in my room with me?" Melanie asked as she led me up the huge winding staircase in the Hans' spacious modern home.

As always I was in total awe of the place. The living room furniture was all black leather, glass, and chrome. Expensive, colorful artwork hung on the plain white walls, lit by individual spotlights. Every rug in the house was white, and they were all perfectly spotless, probably because everyone who walked through the front door had to remove his or her shoes instantly. I looked out from the top of the stairs at the breathtaking view of the ocean and sighed. This was definitely the life.

"Ashley? Are you in there?" Melanie asked.

"Oh, sorry," I said. "Just checking out the

scenery. I'll stay in your room with you."

Melanie grinned. "Cool. I was hoping you'd say that."

There were at least three guest rooms in the house, but I had no problem sharing with Melanie. She had two double beds in her massive room, so I always stayed with her when I slept over on weekends. Besides, crashing in Melanie's room was like staying in a hotel.

The walls of her bedroom were painted a deep dark red, and the beds were decked out in plush, exotic fabrics in purple, gold, and brown. Scratch the hotel thing. Staying there was like staying in a palace. I placed my bags on the second bed just as the door downstairs slammed closed.

"Is that your dad?" I asked, excited.

"I hope so. Otherwise someone just broke in," Melanie joked. "Let's go say hi. I want to tell him that I got costume designer."

I couldn't believe what I was hearing. "You haven't told him yet? You found out last week."

"He was away for a few days, getting things ready for the show," Melanie explained. "He's always really busy this time of year."

From the top of the stairs I could see Mr. Han walking through the living room toward the kitchen. He held a large flat briefcase type of bag in one hand while he flipped through the mail with the other. He was wearing mirrored sunglasses, a white linen shirt open at the collar, and a pair of stylish brown linen pants with sandals. I couldn't help smiling. My dad was rarely seen outside a blue button-down, khakis, and loafers.

"Hey, Dad!" Melanie called out.

Her father stopped in his tracks and looked up as if he was startled. Then he smiled when he saw me and Melanie hit the bottom of the stairs.

"Peaches," he said to Melanie. He looked warmly at me. "I see our houseguest has arrived."

"Hi, Mr. Han," I said, eyeing his portfolio. "Are those your sketches for Fashion Week? May we see them?"

Okay, so I was a little psyched.

Mr. Han laughed. "I like your enthusiasm," he said, leading us into the kitchen. He placed the portfolio on the long chrome-and-glass table. I sat on one of the high stools and reached toward the bag, but Melanie grabbed my arm before I could even touch the leather.

"Dad never shows anyone his sketches before the line debuts. Not even me," Melanie told me. "He thinks it's bad luck."

"Oh," I said, unable to hide my disappoint-ment. I was *dying* to see what was inside that bag.

Mr. Han took a sip of his water and eyed the two of us. "Well, I don't see what the harm would be," he said with a smile. "I'm pretty confident about this show."

My spirits soared as Melanie's jaw dropped. "Are you kidding me?" Melanie said. "Dad, you, like, *live* by superstitions."

"Well, maybe it's time for me to change my ways," Mr. Han said. "Superstitions are for the weak at heart, right, Ashley?"

"You know what they say about breaking habits, Mr. Han," I said, sitting up straight. I would have said pretty much anything to get my eyes on his designs. "There's no day like today."

He pulled the portfolio toward him, and hesi-tated a split second before unzipping it.

Melanie looked at me, her eyes still wide with surprise. "I guess there really *is* a first time for everything," she said, sitting next to me. She flipped her long side-ponytail over one shoulder, and we both sat forward eagerly.

"Exactly," Mr. Han said, unzipping the bag on the table. It opened flat, revealing a beautiful sketch on each side. "Besides, we wouldn't want to make our guest feel unwelcome. She asked to see them, so we should let her see them."

"Wow," I said breathlessly.

I used my fingertips to slide the portfolio toward me. The first sketch was of a willowy girl in a long, asymmetrical ball gown. The skirt hung at various lengths and angles, and I could practically feel how soft the fabric would be, flowing against my skin. It was all I could do to keep from reaching out to touch the drawing.

The second sketch was of a girl in a slim gown in shimmering silver with a long train extending from the skirt. I couldn't even imagine wearing anything so fabulous.

"Dad, these are amazing," Melanie said.

"I'm glad you like them," Mr. Han said, sipping his water. "Ashley? What do you think?"

"They're gorgeous," I replied, flipping to the next page. "I can't wait until the show this weekend so we can see them in person."

"Well, why wait?" Mr. Han said with a shrug. "We're having the first dress rehearsal on Tuesday. You girls should come down."

Melanie's right hand hit the table like an exclamation point. "Dad, are you feeling okay?" she asked.

"I can't invite my daughter and her friend to the fashion show tents?" he asked, chuckling.

"No, you can. You *totally* can," I said, my pulse pounding.

"You just never have before," Melanie said.

"Well, we'll call this a day of firsts, then," he said. "I'd love to hear what you think of the line."

"Oh . . . okay," Melanie said, looking totally freaked. "Thanks."

"I'm going to go make a few phone calls and then we'll do dinner," Mr. Han said, backing out the side door of the kitchen. "Okay?"

"Okay," Melanie said again.

The second Mr. Han was out of the room, I jumped up and threw my arms in the air. "This is so awesome!" I said, hugging Melanie. "See? I knew your life was amazing!"

"Okay, it is not normally like this," Melanie said, pulling back to look at me. "He has never shown me his sketches before the show, and I've only ever been to dress rehearsals when I was too young to be left home alone." She raised her eyebrows at me. "He must like you."

I was beaming. "You think? That's so sweet," I said. "But I doubt it was because of me. It sounds like he wants us both to see his stuff."

"Yeah. I guess it does," Melanie said with a small smile.

"Hey! You didn't tell him about the costume-designer thing," I reminded her.

"Right! Duh!" Melanie said, squeezing her eyes closed and bringing a hand to her forehead. "I totally spaced. I think I went into shock over his showing us his sketches. I'll tell him later."

"Okay," I said. "I can't believe that tomorrow we're going to be hanging out with all those models and designers," I trilled, my skin practically tingling in anticipation. "A-list fabulousness, here we come!"

"You love this applesauce, don't you?" I said to Lucas, hardly even realizing I was baby-talking. "Yes, you do! Yes, you do!"

Lucas laughed at me and dribbled a little sauce down his chin. I quickly picked up a soft cloth napkin and wiped the mess away. So far his high-chair tray was spotless, and he had only a couple of stains on his bib. I had worn my oldest Malibu High T-shirt just in case of projectile food, but it was clean as well. Honestly, at this point I had no idea what Brittany had been talking about. Little Lucas was a perfect gentleman.

"Mary-Kate, you are a dream," Mrs. Bowen said.

The entire Bowen family was hovering behind me as I fed the baby. They had stood by to help me, but I was doing fine on my own. I had figured they would go off after a while to do their own things, but they kept watching me as if I was putting on a play or something.

"I'm usually covered head to toe by now," Brittany added.

"You must have the magic touch, Mary-Kate," Mr. Bowen put in.

"I usually don't," I said, as Lucas swallowed the latest spoonful, laughed, and waved his arms up and down. "Back when Ashley and I used to babysit together, I was always better with the hyper toddlers, and she handled all the babies."

I turned and looked at Lucas again, who was reaching out toward the spoon in my hand as if he wanted more. I scooped a baby-sized bite of food into the spoon and fed it to him.

"Huh. I guess that's changed," I said with a casual shrug. Inside I was feeling quite proud of myself. I was actually good with babies! Who knew?

"Well, you couldn't have picked a better time to come stay with us," Mrs. Bowen said, grabbing an apron off a peg on the wall. "We're catering Paul Han's Fashion Week show and party this weekend, and Brittany's dad and I are going to be crazy busy this week."

"We're going to have tastings and menu meetings . . . and we're going to have to hire a couple of new waiters," Mr. Bowen put in.

"Well, anything I can do to help . . ." I said with a smile. I mean, if the baby was this good, I was more than happy to pitch in and give Brittany and her parents a break.

Brittany pulled up a chair and sat down next to me as I dug out another spoonful for Lucas.

"Really, Mary-Kate, I wish I was videotaping this," Brittany said. "Actually, I wish I had taped all his other feedings so you could see what he's usually like. I'm not kidding. This kid is a psycho."

Lucas giggled and gurgled up a bubble, then laughed when it popped.

"Oh, yeah. He's really scary," I said.

Brittany and I both giggled. "Okay. You're a *cute* psycho," she told her brother, tickling his chubby cheeks with both hands.

Lucas laughed so hard, his eyes closed, and I couldn't stop grinning. I didn't care how much Brittany tried to scare me. So far Lucas was an angel. If this baby was this good with me, this week was going to be tons of fun.

chapter three

That night, while Melanie was washing up in the bathroom, I lay back against the cushy pillows in her extra bed with the new copy of *Mod* magazine open in my lap. There was a whole layout devoted to up-and-coming designers, and right in the center was Melanie's dad. The reporter wrote that Mr. Han had "one of the most unique visions in the industry." Unbelievable. I was reading about the person in the very next room! In *Mod*! How cool was that?

I heard Melanie leave the bathroom and knock on the door of her father's room down the hall.

"Come in!" he said.

"Hey, Dad," I heard Melanie say. "I just wanted to tell you I have some good news."

I put the magazine down and smiled. I knew I

shouldn't be listening in on a private conversation, but I couldn't help it. The house was so huge and open that every conversation echoed off the walls. It wasn't as if I could shut my ears. Besides, Melanie was *so* excited about getting to be the costume designer for the play. I loved to hear her talk about it. She got all giddy.

"What is it, Peaches?" her father asked.

"Well, we're doing this play at school. . . . It's called *Groovin*, and it takes place in the 1970s. And guess what? I got picked to be the costume designer!" Melanie said.

"Really? Honey, that's great!" her father replied.

I grinned and hugged my blanket closer to me. I could just imagine the psyched look on Melanie's face. I knew she really wanted to show her father that she was following in his footsteps.

"It was so cool," she began. "We all had to submit three sketches that showed our ideas for the play. And Mrs. Warren, the art teacher, she encouraged me to do it. I wasn't even going to try until she suggested it. But I still can't believe I got picked."

"That's just great, honey," her father said again.

"So, do you want to see my sketches? I have them in my room," Melanie said.

There was a long pause.

"Dad?"

"I'm sorry, Peaches. What did you say?"

"I . . . uh . . . I asked you if you wanted to see my sketches," Melanie said, her voice a little less excited than it was a second ago.

"Oh, well, can we do it some other time, Melanie?" her father asked. "I'm a bit busy right now."

"Oh. Yeah. I guess," Melanie said.

Now she sounded completely depressed. My heart thumped sadly in my chest. I couldn't believe her dad didn't want to see her drawings. I had seen them, and they were amazing.

"Okay. I guess I'll just . . . see you tomorrow," Melanie said.

There was another pause, and then her dad finally said, "Right. Good night, Peaches."

A door closed, and I picked up my magazine again, pretending to be riveted by an article on the new argyle. I didn't want Melanie to think I was spying on her.

Melanie opened the door to the bedroom and walked in, her eyes trained on the floor. I don't think I'd ever seen her look so lifeless.

"Hey . . . so . . . what time do you get up in the

morning?" I asked her, trying to sound upbeat.

"I set the alarm for seven," she said flatly, climbing into bed.

"Okay, so do you want to watch TV or something, or do you just want to go to sleep?" I asked.

"I just want to go to sleep," she said, reaching for the light next to her bed. "You can stay up and read though. I don't mind."

"That's okay," I said, faking a yawn. "I'm kind of tired, too."

Seeing her like this was so disturbing, I wanted to get her talking, but she turned over with her back to me.

"'Night, Ashley," she said quietly.

"Good night," I replied, flicking off the light next to my bed.

For a minute I just lay there, listening to the sound of my own breathing. I almost didn't want to move because I didn't want to make noise and disturb Melanie, who was clearly upset. Was everything okay with her? I mean, I understood that her dad had basically just blown her off, but, like he said, he was swamped. I was sure that next week, when his show was over, he would be all about seeing Melanie's sketches and talking to her about the play.

I glanced at the clock. It was actually pretty early. I wasn't used to going to bed just yet. I thought about calling Mary-Kate to chat about our first night in our new homes, but I didn't want to annoy Melanie, who obviously wanted to sleep. Plus if I called the Bowens', I might wake up Lucas, which would not be good.

With a sigh I scrunched down lower in my bed and closed my eyes to try to sleep. I just hoped Melanie would feel better in the morning.

I woke up suddenly in the middle of the night to the sound of an inhuman screeching. My breath caught in my throat as I sat up straight on the cot the Bowens had pulled out for me. In the bed a few feet away Brittany stirred in her sleep and sighed.

"Brittany? What is that? Is that your brother?" I asked, unable to believe that anything that small could make a noise that large. I was surprised dogs weren't barking in distress all over the neighborhood.

"Oh, yeah. That's him," she said, staring up at the ceiling. "Just call him Lucas 'The Lungs' Bowen."

"Is he okay? Is he sick?" I asked, rubbing the sleep from my eyes.

"No, he's fine," Brittany said with a yawn.

I scrunched up my face as the crying intensified. How could Brittany be so casual about this?

"He sounds like he's being tortured," I said. "Aren't your parents going to go in there?"

"No. They're trying to get him to sleep through the night," Brittany said.

Huh? No one was going to be sleeping through the night with that kind of racket going on. Least of all Lucas. I could just imagine the pained look on his face, the tears streaming down his cheeks. It was so awful. How could his parents ignore him this way?

"Okay, explain to me why this is good," I said, closing my eyes against a particularly sad wail.

Brittany sat up and turned on the light next to her bed. I blinked at the sudden brightness and tried to focus my watery eyes on her.

"It's called Ferberizing the baby," she said.

"Excuse me?" I said. "Ferber what?"

"Ferberizing. I know it sounds like something out of a *Star Wars* movie, but apparently this guy named Dr. Ferber came up with this theory," Brittany explained. "Every night you let the baby cry a little bit longer before going in and checking on him. The idea is to get him used to putting himself back to sleep. So you're allowed to stand in the doorway and let him know you're there, but you're not allowed to pick him up or rock him or anything. Nothing that would help put him to sleep. This way, eventually he'll figure out a way to put *himself* out. My parents have been gradually getting farther and farther from the crib each night and they've finally worked up to not going in there at all."

I blinked. "Interesting theory."

"It's not just a theory. They have friends who've done this. And he really will stop soon." She yawned. "Okay, I'm going back to sleep now," Brittany said, turning off the light again.

"You can *sleep* through this?" I said, baffled.

"The first cry usually wakes me up, but then I fall back to sleep," Brittany said. "I'm used to it. G'night, Mary-Kate."

"'Night," I said.

I lay back, my eyes wide open as I stared at the ceiling. This was unreal. Lucas's cries sounded as if they could take down the whole house. How could anyone sleep through such a thing?

I waited a few minutes, struggling against the urge to go into his room and check on him. I didn't want to go against the Bowens' rules, but this was crazy. I mean, this could not be normal crying. What if Brittany's parents were wrong? What if he actually had some huge, high fever or something, and no one went in there to help him? Or, worse, what if he were hurt? From the sound of his screams you'd think something awful had happened.

"Brittany?" I whispered finally. I mean, we were already up. We might as well talk to pass the time.

She didn't answer. She did, in fact, let out a light snore. I couldn't believe it, but she was really in a deep sleep.

I sighed and thought of Ashley, lying in Melanie's big soft guest bed, sleeping like a baby.

Lucas let out another screech, and I remembered. Apparently babies *didn't* sleep. That expression really needed to be changed.

The baby was sobbing uncontrollably now, and I couldn't take it anymore. I felt like a jerk lying there while he was so miserable. Plus I was never going to get any sleep at this rate. I tossed the covers aside, slid my feet into my slippers, and tiptoed into the hallway.

I crept past the Bowens' bedroom and saw that the door to Lucas's nursery was ajar. Pushing it open quietly, I slipped inside. Lucas quieted down the second he saw me. He was standing up in his blue and white onesie pajamas, clutching the side of the crib. His lips were still quivering as I approached him, and his face was wet with tears. His curly black hair was plastered to his forehead with sweat. He held out his arms toward me.

"Hey . . . you're okay," I whispered to him, picking him up.

His big eyes looked up at me hopefully. I checked his forehead, and he didn't feel unusually hot or feverish. He must have just sweat from all the exertion of screaming at the top of his lungs.

"Everything's okay now," I told him, bouncing him up and down. "Aunt Mary-Kate is here now. It's time for you to go to sleep. . . ."

chapter four

I woke up on Monday morning and blinked a few times, looking around in confusion. Where was I? This was not my room. This was not even Brittany's room. Then I heard Lucas giggle, and I realized what had happened. I had fallen asleep on the love seat in his room. Last night after finally, *finally* getting him to shut his eyes, I had sat down to watch him for a little while, just in case he started crying again. Apparently a little while had turned into a major snooze fest.

My neck cried out in pain as I lifted my head from a small throw pillow. Curled up in a ball with my head tilted up had not been the best way to sleep. My entire body ached.

"Hey, Lucas," I said, pushing myself up with a yawn. "How did *you* sleep?"

As I was standing, the door to the room opened, and in walked Brittany's mom and dad, all dressed and ready for work. They were smiling bright morning smiles—until they saw me.

"Mary-Kate? What are you doing in here?" Brittany's mom asked, her brow knitting.

"Oh, I . . . um . . . I fell asleep on the love seat," I said, my face heating up. Somewhere in the back of my tired mind I realized that I was not supposed to be in the baby's room.

"When did you come in here?" Mr. Bowen asked.

Lucas laughed and held his arms out toward his mom. Mrs. Bowen walked over to the crib and picked Lucas up, giving me a second to formulate my answer. But there wasn't much I could say to get myself out of the situation. They had caught me red-handed.

"I came in last night. When Lucas was crying," I said finally, biting my lip. "I'm sorry. I know I wasn't supposed to. But he just sounded so miserable. . . ."

Mr. Bowen sighed, which only made me feel worse.

"Mary-Kate, honey, I know you were just trying to help, but coming in here doesn't help Lucas or us," Mrs. Bowen explained gently. "Last night when Lucas stopped crying, we thought he was making progress—that he had finally learned how to put himself to sleep."

"But your coming in here may have actually set *back* his progress," Mr. Bowen added.

"Really? Just one night can set him back?" I asked.

"Yes, just one night," Mr. Bowen said. "We do appreciate the effort, Mary-Kate, but—"

"I shouldn't do it again," I said with a nod. I felt like such a moron. I hadn't even been here one whole day, and already the Bowens were upset with me. "I understand. And I really am sorry."

"It's okay," Mrs. Bowen said. "Living with a baby is hard work. And trust me, listening to him cry is the hardest thing. It breaks your heart, but we have to try it. Okay?"

"Okay," I said. "I guess I'll just go get ready for school."

I walked out of the room all achy and tired and feeling guilty. What a way to start the day.

❁

The smell of cooking bacon woke me up on Monday morning and my stomach was grumbling before I even realized where I was. At first I thought my dad had decided to make a big breakfast. He sometimes did that so that the whole family could sit down and eat together in the morning. But when I opened my eyes, I realized my dad couldn't be cooking for us. I was at Melanie's house. Maybe *her* dad was cooking!

I glanced at her bed and found that it was already made, so I jumped up and started getting ready for school. I took a little extra time in the shower, playing with the different settings on the state-of-the-art showerhead and trying out all the different, nature-scented body washes. Even the towels in the bathroom were bigger, thicker, and softer than any I had ever used before. I felt as if I was staying at a resort, not a friend's house.

All through my teeth-brushing and hair-styling, amazing smells wafted up from the kitchen. I could hardly wait to get down there. But when I finally walked into the room, it wasn't Mr. Han in front of the stove, but Melanie.

"Hey!" I said brightly. "Something smells amazing."

"Omelets, bacon, and toast," Melanie said with a smile as she expertly folded an omelet in the pan in front of her. "You hungry?"

"Definitely. But you didn't have to go to all this

32

trouble," I told her. Wanting to help, I brought a plate loaded with buttered toast slices to the table and started pouring out orange juice from the pitcher in the fridge.

"I wanted to," Melanie said. "Not just for my guest, but for my dad, too. He's got a long day today, so I thought he could use the protein."

My grin widened. "You're such a good daughter," I said.

"I know," she replied with a shrug and a smile.

Just then her father walked in looking all distracted as his hands went in and out of his pockets.

"Hey, Daddy!" Melanie said.

"Have you girls seen my keys?" he asked.

"Uh . . . no," Melanie said. "But I can look for them while you eat breakfast. I made omelets." She held up the pan with the perfectly folded tomato-and-pepper omelet inside.

Mr. Han looked up at her and seemed to notice the food for the first time. I don't know how he could have missed it, considering that the entire house was filled with the unbelievable smells.

"Oh, Peaches, I don't have time for a big breakfast this morning," he said. "I'll just grab a bagel at the beach."

Melanie's face fell, and she placed the pan back

on the cooling burner. I glanced at Mr. Han. He was still searching for his keys and didn't notice his daughter's disappointment.

"Ah! There they are!" Mr. Han said, grabbing his keys out from under the newspaper on the counter. "Thanks for making breakfast, Melanie. I'm sure you and Ashley will enjoy it."

He planted a kiss on top of her head, snagged a slice of toast from the table, and headed out. "Have a good day!" he called out from the living room.

"You, too!" Melanie called back.

But the door had slammed before the second word was even out of her mouth.

Mary-Kate and I were the first ones dressed and out of the locker room at gym class on Monday. We were playing soccer, and we all had to walk to the field behind the school. Mary-Kate and I had decided to get out there early so we could catch each other up on our new living situations. As we started up the hill toward the field, the only other people around were the teachers and a couple of the guys, who were way ahead of us.

"So! What's it like living in Melanie's mansion?"

Mary-Kate asked excitedly as she tied her dark hair back from her face.

"It's unbelievable," I said. "Her dad just bought this new flat-screen TV. You push a button, and it actually comes up out of a cabinet."

"Cool!" Mary-Kate said. "And did you sleep in her guest bed with all those cushy pillows and those soft, soft sheets?"

"Oh, yeah," I replied. "I slept like a rock."

Mary-Kate sighed. "I'm so jealous."

"Why? You didn't sleep well?" I asked, kicking a pebble off the path in front of me.

"Let's just say that Lucas likes to cry. A lot. In the wee hours of the morning," Mary-Kate said.

"Ouch," I replied. "That can't be fun."

"Even worse? I went in there to calm him down, and the Bowens got mad at me," Mary-Kate said. "It turns out they're teaching him to put himself to sleep, and I messed up the works."

"That stinks," I said. "Sounds like you didn't have the best first night."

"Oh, no! Don't get me wrong," Mary-Kate said, her eyes widening slightly. "Lucas is so cute and the Bowens are really nice. Plus they made the most amazing barbecue dinner last night. I mean, it was like *gourmet* barbecue."

"I guess that's how you eat when you're living with career caterers," I said.

"What about Mr. Han? How's he?" Mary-Kate asked as we reached edge of the soccer field.

"He's very nice. He even invited me to a dress rehearsal at the beach tomorrow afternoon," I said.

"Sweet!" Mary-Kate replied.

"I know!" I glanced over my shoulder. The rest of the class was still yards behind us. "The only thing is . . . he's really busy, and I think Melanie's feeling kind of upset."

"How come?" Mary-Kate asked.

"It's hard to explain," I said, crossing my arms over my chest. "It's, like, he doesn't really have time to talk to her and he didn't eat breakfast with us this morning. And I can tell she's hurt by it. I don't know, it's just kind of . . . uncomfortable."

"Wow," Mary-Kate said. "Who knew? Do you think that she wants him to—"

I noticed that the group was catching up to us, with Brittany, Melanie, and Lauren at the front of the pack. I quickly shushed Mary-Kate, who pressed her lips together. We were going to have to continue this conversation another time.

"Hey! You guys ready to play a little soccer?" I

said, clapping my hands as I turned to face our friends.

"Since when are you all psyched up for gym?" Brittany asked, eyeing me as if I was nuts.

Since I didn't want to get caught talking about you guys, I answered silently, glancing at Melanie.

But I just smiled and shrugged. I knew I shouldn't feel guilty about our conversation. After all, Mary-Kate and I were obviously going to talk about what was going on in our lives. But I had a feeling that our friends might not see it that way, and that had been a bit of a close call. Maybe living with our friends was going to be a little more complicated than we had thought.

chapter five

"This is incredible," I said excitedly. It was Tuesday afternoon, and Melanie and I had just walked into the tent where her father's fashion show would be held. It was a huge white canvas structure set up on the beach, smack in the center of a dozen others just like it. Each designer had his or her own tent, which were identical from the outside, but inside the designers could decorate however they wanted.

Mr. Han's tent was beautiful. Understated but beautiful. Hanging from the wooden rafters were dozens of canvas orbs in red, orange, and yellow. They were all different sizes, from about eight inches to two feet wide, and each had a light inside. The T-shaped runway at the head of the tent was lacquered black and was lined with little shoots of bamboo. Lights of all colors flashed at the stage from above, and a DJ was spinning from his booth in the corner. He kept trying out different tracks, so every few minutes the music switched from hip-hop to dance to techno to pop.

Workers bustled around, setting up chairs along the runway and placing tables farther back in the room where I assumed drinks and finger foods would be served. I looked around to see if Brittany's parents were there, but I didn't spot them. All I saw were tall, beautiful models strutting around and men dressed in black with little microphone sets on their heads, barking orders to one another across the room.

"Is it always this intense?" I asked Melanie as we wove our way toward the stage.

"I have no idea. I haven't been to a dress rehearsal since I was in diapers," Melanie said.

We had come straight from school, so we dropped our backpacks on a chair near the runway and headed backstage. I still couldn't believe I was there. How many people got to see how a fashion show really worked?

"Omigosh! Is that Molly St. John?" I whispered, a tingle of surprise rushing over my skin. Sitting not three feet away was a very familiar-looking woman with the longest legs I had ever seen in person. Her red hair was tied back in a ponytail and she wore a casual track suit, but she still looked as if she belonged in a fashion magazine. She sipped from a water bottle and looked fairly bored while an older lady stood next to her, arguing with one of the men in black.

Melanie grabbed my arm. "It is!" she said. "My dad didn't tell me she was in his show this year. She's, like, the most famous model in the world!"

We gripped hands for a second and then both realized how silly we looked. Separating, we tried to play it cool as we walked by Molly.

"Molly *must* be the last model out," the older woman was saying to the young man. "She is a superstar. She will not be buried in the middle of the line."

I saw Molly roll her eyes and I smiled. The older woman must be her agent. But Molly didn't really seem to care about where she was in the show. Then she looked up, and her eyes met mine. She caught me smiling and smiled back.

"Hi!" I said, feeling I had to say something. "You're Molly St. John. I mean, wow. I can't believe you're Molly St. John."

What? What was I saying?

"Always nice to meet a fan," Molly said casually.

"You, too. I mean, nice to meet you, too," I blabbered.

Melanie had to grab me and drag me away before I said something else. So much for playing it cool. But I couldn't help it. The woman had her picture in every magazine I had ever picked up in my life. I was in the presence of greatness.

"Hey, there's my dad," Melanie said as we walked into one of the dressing rooms.

He was standing at the back of the room, staring at a model in a white dress. His hands were over his mouth, and he kept shaking his head.

"Turn. Turn for me again," he said.

The model did as she was told. It was a gorgeous piece. It had wide shoulders and a dramatic low back. The skirt was sleek and above the knee. The whole thing was a beautiful, gleaming white.

"Something's off. What is it?" Mr. Han said. "There's just something off."

"Hey, Dad," Melanie said quietly as we approached. "Is this a bad time?"

"Hi, Peaches. Hello, Ashley," he replied, glancing our way. "Look at this outfit," he said, gesturing toward the model distractedly. "It needs something. What does it need?"

I wasn't sure if he was really asking us or just sort of talking to himself. The model walked a few feet away and turned again, allowing us all to take in her ensemble.

"Maybe it's too much of one color?" Melanie suggested, glancing from the white boots to the white dress to the white earrings. "You could add a colorful belt. Or a scarf."

"No, no, no," Mr. Han said quickly, shaking his head. "I love the elegant line of the dress. A scarf or a belt would just muck it up."

Melanie flushed and shrugged as if she was embarrassed. "It was just an idea."

"What about taking the boots off?" I suggested.

Mr. Han blinked. "The boots?"

"Yeah, I mean, they're nice boots and all, but they're kind of clunky with the dress," I explained. "She could wear a pair of white heels or sandals, and it would be a lot sleeker."

The model looked at Mr. Han for direction and he nodded. "Yes, let's try it. Take off the boots. Corinne, get me those white slingbacks from this morning, would you?"

"Sure," a girl with long dark hair said, springing away from a wall and rushing off.

Another girl with a measuring tape around her

neck and three pencils sticking out of the bun in her hair rushed forward to help the model with the zippers on the boots. Moments later Corinne returned with a pair of strappy shoes. She placed them on the floor in front of the model, who slipped her feet into them.

"Ah! That is much better!" Mr. Han said with a huge grin. "Ashley, thank you so much." He walked over to us and enveloped Melanie and me in a group hug. "I'm so glad you two came today."

Then he walked off with the model to bring her out for a test walk on the stage. I turned to Melanie, all grins. I couldn't believe I had just helped a major designer with an accessory dilemma! But Melanie's face was hard as stone. Instantly a little ball of guilt formed in my stomach.

Maybe chiming in with a solution after Mr. Han shot down Melanie's idea had not been the best idea.

Tuesday night, after I called my parents to check in, Brittany and I sat on the couch in her living room with a bowl of popcorn between us. Neither one of us had touched a single kernel. We were too mesmerized by the television. Our favorite show, *Newport Beach*, was on, and tonight was a big episode. They had been showing teaser commercials all last week, and we were really excited to see it. Apparently tonight was the night Regina might tell Brad how she really felt about him.

"She's going to dump him. I just know it," Brittany said.

"No! Please! She's totally in love with him," I replied.

Two of the lesser characters were on the screen just then, arguing over which one was going to get to ask Andrea to the prom. They cut the scene just as the two guys were about to start a fistfight, and there were Regina and Brad.

"Oh! This is it!" Brittany said, sitting forward in her seat.

I was on the edge of the couch as well. This was the moment we had been waiting for ever since the show started back in September. Everyone wanted to know if Regina and Brad were finally going to get together.

"You wanted to talk to me?" Brad said, those beautiful blue eyes of his filled with longing.

"Yes, Brad," Regina said, twirling a lock of her dark hair around her finger. *"I know I've kept you waiting a long time, and it isn't fair. I asked you here to tell you—"*

At that exact second Lucas started crying in the playpen behind the couch. He screamed so loudly I nearly jumped out of my skin. In fact, he screamed so loudly that he drowned out every last word of Regina's speech. Brittany and I both whipped around to see if he was alright, which he was, and by the time I looked at the screen again, it had gone to commercial.

"Oh, Lucas! What's wrong?" Brittany cooed, walking around the couch to pick him up.

My jaw was on the floor. I couldn't believe we had missed it. We had missed Regina's speech to Brad. It was only *the* moment every teenager in America had been waiting for all year long!

Brittany laid Lucas down on the couch and checked his diaper, which was clean.

"Where's his bottle?" I asked, snapping out of my *Newport Beach* trance when I saw Lucas's tears. "Maybe he's hungry."

Brittany went back to the playpen for his bottle, which was half full, but he batted it away, still crying.

"Maybe he had a nightmare or something," Brittany said.

"Here, let me try," I offered, picking him up.

I bounced him on my hip and talked to him,

but he just kept crying. We tried to give him his Binky, but he wouldn't have it. Brittany found a rattle in his playpen and shook it for him, but that didn't work either. Even his favorite teddy bear didn't chill him out. Three commercials had come and gone, and I was on the verge of begging him to calm down so I could see what happened when the show came back.

"You know, there is one thing that pretty much always works," Brittany said, her hands on her hips.

"What?" I asked as Lucas grabbed my hair and pulled.

"The Snuggly Wugglies video," Brittany said.

She pulled a colorful tape out of a stack next to the TV and popped it into the VCR. Just as the announcer said, "*And now, back to* Newport Beach," the screen went blue, and then a bunch of little red, yellow, and blue shapes started bounding across the screen.

Brittany took Lucas from me and sat down on the floor with him, facing him toward the screen. It took about two seconds for him to stop crying.

I dropped onto the couch, stunned. I was happy that Lucas was happy, but I couldn't believe that instead of watching Regina and Brad in the biggest moment of their lives, I was watching the Snuggly Wugglies. Little cartwheeling cartoon shapes had nothing on the romance of the decade.

Then Lucas laughed and pointed at the screen. His arms shook up and down in happiness, and he clapped. Soon I found myself smiling, and I joined Brittany and Lucas on the floor. At least the baby was happy. But as I watched the minutes tick away on the cable box's clock and realized my show was ending, I let out a sigh. Tomorrow everyone would be talking about *Newport Beach* and I would be the only one who had no idea what was going on. Maybe having a little brother wasn't all it was cracked up to be.

chapter six

Melanie and I were hanging out in the living room that night, watching *Newport Beach* on the big-screen TV. We were waiting for her father to get home with dinner, but neither one of us had mentioned him in at least an hour. I had a feeling Melanie was anxious that he hadn't come home yet, so I didn't want to say anything that would make her worry more. Then, during a commercial break, my stomach growled so loudly, we both heard it over the TV. Melanie looked at me, and we laughed.

Unfortunately, after the laugh came an uncomfortable silence. *Newport Beach* was ending, which meant it was nine o'clock. I was used to eating at around seven. If we didn't get some food soon, I was going to start chewing on one of the leather throw pillows. Not really, but I *was* think-ing about all those cartoons I'd seen in my life where something similar happened. Like when some hungry character looks at his best friend and sees a batch of cookies instead.

"Do you want to try his cell again?" I asked.

"I guess I should," Melanie said. "I don't know what's keeping him. He said he would be home with sushi at eight."

She picked up the cordless phone, which she had kept nearby all night, and hit the REDIAL button. We waited a second, and then she rolled her eyes.

"Voice mail," she said, hanging up. She placed the phone down on the glass-topped coffee table. "I already left two messages, so . . ."

"Well, maybe we should just make ourselves something to eat," I suggested, sitting up a bit. "I'm sure he just got held up, and he wouldn't want us sitting here hungry."

"No. He'll be here," Melanie said. "He'll be upset if he spends all that money on food and then we're not hungry. Maybe we should just have a snack or—"

The phone rang and Melanie pounced on it. "It's him!" she announced, checking the caller ID.

I grinned in relief. Maybe he was just calling to

see what we wanted to eat. In fifteen minutes he would be home, and we would be pigging out on salmon-skin rolls. My stomach let out another grumble at the thought.

"What? But, Dad . . ." Melanie said.

She glanced at me and walked out of the room with the phone. My first instinct was to follow her, but then I heard her lower her voice and realized she didn't want me to hear. Now a new discomfort joined the hunger pangs in my stomach. Melanie was avoiding me. I thought we told each other almost everything.

"Okay. Okay, fine," I heard Melanie say, her voice growing louder again. "Yes. I'll see you later."

The phone beep echoed into the room, and Melanie walked in a second later. She crossed her arms over her chest, still holding the phone in one hand, and smiled a tight little smile.

"He has to stay late," she said. "He had his phone off for the last couple of hours because he was in a meeting with his publicity team."

"Oh. Well, that's okay," I said, trying to ignore the mixture of sorrow and sympathy in my chest. I could tell Melanie was upset, so I decided it was up to me to be upbeat. It wasn't a big deal, really. Sometimes my dad had to work late, too.

"So," I said, walking past her into the kitchen. "What do you want to do for dinner?"

"At this point I think microwave dinners are all that's on the menu," Melanie said, replacing the phone on its cradle. "Sorry. I know you were looking forward to sushi. I can't believe he called so late."

"Trust me, it's fine," I said, grabbing the handle on the freezer door. "Let's see what we've got."

My jaw almost dropped when I looked inside the freezer. There were stacks upon stacks of frozen dinners. Everything from pot pies to Chinese to pasta dishes. It looked as if Melanie ate a lot of insta-meals. Was she really left at home alone so often? And, if so, why didn't I know about it before now?

"So, how do you like living with us so far?" Mrs. Bowen asked me as she placed little Lucas on the changing table in his nursery later that night. On the shelf behind it were a dozen bottles, everything from baby powder to oil to moisturizer to rash-relief cream. Apparently babies needed even more products than a teenager did!

I was flipping through a tiny book called *My Little Lamb*.

"I like it," I said with a smile. "It's not half as crazy as Brittany told me it would be."

Maybe about a third as crazy, I thought to myself. After all, Lucas wasn't a terror, and my life hadn't been *completely* turned upside down. There were just little kinks here and there.

"That's good," Mrs. Bowen said with a smile. "I was a little worried it would be overwhelming for someone who's never lived with a baby."

"Clearly you've never met my sister. Talk about high maintenance," I joked.

Mrs. Bowen laughed, which made Lucas laugh.

I couldn't help grinning. Apparently I was very entertaining!

Mrs. Bowen peeled the tabs off Lucas's diaper, which, luckily was not one of the poopy-smelly ones, and tossed it into the trash bin next to the table. Lucas giggled and grabbed for a lock of his mom's curly hair.

At that moment the phone rang. Mr. Bowen and Brittany had run out to get some ice cream for all of us, so there was no one around to get it.

"Want me to . . . ?" I offered, taking a step toward the door.

"Actually, one of my chefs is flying back from New York, and he's supposed to check in tonight,"

Mrs. Bowen said. "Can you finish up in here while I get that?"

"Uh . . . sure," I said, as she handed me the naked baby.

"Thanks," Mrs. Bowen said, jogging from the room. "I'll be right back."

I held Lucas away from me, thinking of all the movies I'd seen where the baby suddenly decided to pee all over the unsuspecting babysitter. Then I laid him back down on the table.

Okay, diapering. This had never been my talent. I knew that the diaper companies were making these things easier and easier to work with, but somehow I could never get them quite right. But if I was ever going to master the skill, it had to be now. I could hear Mrs. Bowen chatting on the phone down the hall. Lucas looked up at me expectantly. Suddenly I felt exactly as nervous as I had the day I took my driver's test.

"I can do this," I whispered to myself. I grabbed a diaper from the shelf directly under the tabletop and flipped it open.

Okay . . . which is the back, and which is the front? I thought. That was always my first problem. Then I saw a line of little ducks printed in a band across one side of the diaper. Aha! That had to be the front. Thank you, diaper manufacturers of the world!

I laid the diaper down open on the table, then picked up little Lucas and placed him in the center. At least I thought it was the center. It was kind of hard to tell with him squirming all over the place.

"Come on, help me out here, Luc," I said, glancing over my shoulder at the empty hall.

He didn't seem to want to sit still, though. I tried to hold him in place with one hand while ripping open the sticky diaper tabs with the other. The first one took a few attempts to open, so I did the second one like a Band-Aid—quick and painless. And the entire tab came right off in my hand.

"Oh, no!" I cried. Lucas cracked up laughing.

I picked him up, shoved the ruined diaper into the garbage can and tried again.

"Okay, Lucas. Just lie still for one second while Aunt Mary-Kate gets this diaper on," I pleaded.

"Everything okay in here?" Mrs. Bowen whispered.

I glanced behind me, and she was standing in the doorway with one hand over the phone's mouthpiece.

"Yeah! Just fine!" I replied with a wide smile.

She nodded and walked off again.

This time Lucas lay still. I was able to use both hands to carefully open the tabs. I folded the diaper over his belly, fixed the tabs to the front of the diaper, and sighed in relief.

"Second time's the charm," I said, lifting him up.

The diaper slipped right off his legs and hit the floor at my feet.

I groaned and grabbed another diaper, flipping it open on the table. I was about to place Lucas down for a third try when he grabbed my hair and pulled—*hard*. I shouted and groped for his rattle to distract him. Instead I knocked over the baby oil, which popped open and spilled all over the new diaper, making a slimy mess.

I felt tears of frustration sting my eyes. Well, maybe it was frustration mixed with pain. That Lucas had some serious grip! I finally put him down again, pried his little fists from my hair, and deposited the second and third diapers in the trash can.

"Okay, maybe the *fourth* time is the charm," I muttered, though I was pretty sure the saying was about the third time, not the second *or* the fourth. I was grasping at straws here.

I took out another diaper, opened it on the

table, and told myself I could do this. Lucas sat still this time—maybe he sensed my panic—and I fastened the tabs a little tighter than I had before. When I picked him up again, I held my breath. The diaper didn't fall off. The duckies were on the front. There were no rips in sight. I'd done it!

"Sorry about that," Mrs. Bowen said, walking back into the room just then. She reached for Lucas, who immediately put his arms out for her. He probably wanted to get away from the incompetent diaperer as quickly as possible.

"There's my boy!" Mrs. Bowen said, rubbing her nose against Lucas's. "Nice job, Mary-Kate," she said, inspecting my work. "We should have you over more often."

I grinned back at her, feeling like a big faker. She thought I was this talented, competent babysitter. Little did she know I had wasted three whole diapers and half a cup of baby oil perfecting my "nice job."

This having-a-little-brother thing was a lot more work than I'd thought it would be!

chapter seven

The next day after school Ashley and I met at Click Café to catch up with each other and do homework. At lunch with Melanie, Brittany, and Lauren, I had heard all about the dress rehearsal, but I was sure there were still some things my sister and I could only talk about in private. I was concentrating on my chemistry textbook when she slid into the seat across from me.

"Wow, when you said you wanted to do a little homework, you really wanted to do homework," she said, looking at all the open books and notebooks around me on the table.

"Just trying to catch up a bit," I said, closing the chemistry text and setting it aside. "I don't know how Brittany gets any work done."

"Oh, so the baby *is* driving you crazy," Ashley

said, grabbing an onion ring from the basket.

"Not even!" I replied. "It's just that when he's around, you want to play with him all the time."

"I know what you mean," Ashley replied. "I want to play in Melanie's closet all the time."

I laughed and took a sip of my soda. "So are things a little better with her dad?" I asked.

"A little. He's not exactly the sit-down, eat-a-meal-with-the-family-and-catch-up-on-the-day type of guy. And I kind of think Melanie wishes he was," she replied. "What about Lucas's crying? Did he do it again last night?"

"Oh, yeah," I replied. "He didn't cry for as long, I don't think, but I had to wrap a blanket *and* a pillow around my head to muffle the noise."

Ashley sighed. "Maybe Brittany and Melanie were right. Maybe their lives *aren't* the greatest."

"I don't know. You did get to meet Molly St. John yesterday, and I did learn how to diaper a baby," I said. Then I narrowed my eyes. "Huh. Somehow I think you got the better deal here."

Ashley laughed and pulled out her chemistry book. "Come on," she said. "Let's get to work."

"Okay, I like math as much as the next person, but fifty problems for homework? I think that can be classified as torture," Melanie said that night.

"Call Amnesty International," I joked, looking up from my notebook.

Melanie and I both laughed, and I tried not to glance at the silver clock that hung above the stove in the kitchen. We were in the same math class, so I had saved my problems for tonight when we could do them together. We were working at the table because we couldn't both fit at Melanie's desk, but being in the kitchen was making me a little tense. After all, for the second night in a row we were waiting for her father to come home with dinner. He had promised Melanie that he would make last night's missed meal up to her. All I could do was hope that he would keep his promise.

Finally, without my even realizing it, my eyes traveled to the clock. It was 7:30.

"I'm sure he'll be here any minute," Melanie said automatically. Apparently she was looking at the clock a lot, too.

I heard a car in the driveway and sat up straight.

Melanie's whole face brightened and her smile practically lit up the room. I could tell she was relieved, and so was I. The last thing I wanted was for her to get upset again the way she had the night before. She was one of my best friends. I wanted her to be happy, like she was just then.

"See?" she said.

I grinned in response.

The front door opened, and Melanie was on her feet. She went directly to the cabinets and started pulling out plates. Following her lead, I cleared up our books and stacked them off to the side.

"Hey, Dad!" Melanie called out before he was even in the room.

"Hey, Peaches!" he called back.

I heard him in his office, rummaging around for something. My spirits drooped. If he had come home with sushi, he probably would have come directly to the kitchen.

After a couple of minutes Mr. Han walked into the kitchen and paused when he saw me and Melanie setting the table. We both glanced at his hands. No brown bags filled with food. All he was carrying were a couple of folders.

Mr. Han's face fell. So did Melanie's. I'm pretty sure mine did, too.

"Oh, Peaches, I completely forgot," he said.

"Again?" Melanie asked.

"I'm sorry. It's just been so crazy down at the

show," her father said. "We're reworking the lighting scheme, and I . . . "

He trailed off and looked at her, almost as if he was begging for forgiveness.

"And you have to get back," Melanie said, setting a ceramic plate on the table with a little clang.

"I'm sorry, Melanie . . . Ashley," he said. "It just can't be avoided. Why don't you girls order a pizza?" he suggested, reaching into his pocket and pulling out a wad of cash. He handed a couple of twenties to Melanie. "You can get some of that garlic bread you like, too. And dessert."

Melanie took the money, but she couldn't even look at her father. My heart completely went out to her. She looked so forlorn.

"We'll do sushi another night," Mr. Han said. Then he gave Melanie a quick kiss on the forehead, raised one hand at me in a wave, and hurried out.

"I don't believe this," Melanie said, dropping heavily into her chair and avoiding my gaze.

"I'm sure it's just Fashion Week," I said, hoping to make her feel better. "He's stressed out. People forget things when they're stressed out."

"Even promises they make to their daughters?" Melanie asked.

"Come on, Mel," I said, sitting in the chair catty-cornered from hers. "I bet when the fashion show is over this weekend, things will go back to normal."

"This *is* normal," Melanie said, her eyes flashing as she finally looked at me. "I guess I thought that if we had a guest staying with us that he would . . . I don't know . . . make more of an effort to come home."

"I don't understand," I said.

"It's not just Fashion Week, Ashley," Melanie told me. "He's hardly ever around."

"No! I can't believe that," I said, trying to stay positive. "Your dad is so sweet!"

"Well, you're not the one who lives here, are you?" Melanie snapped. "You have no idea what you're talking about."

I sat back in my chair as Melanie pushed hers away from the table with a loud scrape. I felt as if I had been slapped. Melanie had never snapped at me before. *Never.* She must be really upset.

As Melanie grabbed a menu from a stack near the refrigerator and started dialing the phone, I couldn't even move. For the first time I realized that maybe Melanie didn't have as fabulous a life as Mary-Kate and I had always believed. And for the first time I started to wonder if our friendship was going to survive this living arrangement.

❀

The wind whipped my hair around my face as I finished off my last bite of chicken and sat back. Mr. and Mrs. Bowen had cooked up another awesome meal, and we had all eaten at the table on their deck overlooking the backyard. Even though we were a couple of blocks away from the beach, I could hear the waves crashing onto the shore. In a few days the fashion shows would be taking place just a short walk away from where I was sitting.

"I can't believe you guys are so close to the Fashion Week site," I said, leaning back.

"We should hang out in the front yard while the shows are going on," Brittany suggested. "Maybe some famous people will drive by."

"Good idea," Mr. Bowen said as he stood to clear his place. "You can shout to them and talk up the food at the Paul Han show. Get us some new clients."

"Very funny, Dad," Brittany said.

"Thanks for dinner, Mr. and Mrs. Bowen," I said, standing as well. "It was amazing. As always."

"Thank you, Mary-Kate. Glad you liked it," Mr. Bowen replied. "I tried out a new recipe tonight, and I wasn't sure how it would go over."

"Well, whatever you did to that chicken, it was the best I've ever tasted," I told him.

"And the mashed potatoes?" Brittany put in, covering her stomach with her free hand. "I think I had thirds *and* fourths."

"Then I won't tell you that it was really mashed cauliflower," her father said.

Brittany shot straight up in her chair. "Cauliflower!"

Mr. Bowen laughed as we all walked into the kitchen to clean up. Mrs. Bowen lifted Lucas out of his high chair and hoisted him onto her hip.

"I think I'll give this one his bottle and put him to bed," she said. "Do we have any clean ones?"

"Mary-Kate and I washed a few this afternoon," Brittany told her mom, heading for the sink with her plate.

"I can put the bottle together, Mrs. Bowen," I offered, noticing how tired she looked. "Why don't you take him up, and I'll be there in a sec?"

"Thanks. That would be great," she replied. "Make sure it's warm. He does better with a warm bottle."

"Got it," I replied.

I had seen Brittany and her parents fill the

bottle and warm it up in the microwave dozens of times. It looked easy enough, and I was more than ready to prove that I was still big-sister material after the diaper disaster. Not that anyone else knew that I had wasted three diapers, but I did. At this point I had something to prove to myself.

Brittany and Mr. Bowen went back to the deck to finish clearing the table. I filled one of Lucas's bottles with milk and put it in the microwave for a minute and a half. That worked for coffee, so I figured it would work for a bottle, too. The beeper went off, and I put the top on the bottle.

"Be right back!" I called to Brittany and her dad. Then I headed upstairs.

Even though I had covered my ears the night before to block out Lucas's crying, I was pretty sure he hadn't cried as long as he had the night before. I liked to think that he was learning. Maybe he had found his bottle in the crib on his own and calmed himself back to sleep. Whether this was true or not, I was proud of the little guy, and so was the rest of the family. It was kind of cool to be there while he was learning something so important.

Plus I was glad that my first night's mistake hadn't set his progress back *too* much. Maybe tonight he would actually sleep through the night. A girl could dream!

At the top of the stairs I stepped over the protective gate that was always up to keep Lucas from tumbling down the steps. I walked into the nursery, where Mrs. Bowen was walking around the room with Lucas in her arms. She was whispering something to him, and he was looking up at her with a wide-eyed smile as if she was the only woman on earth. I guess, when you're a baby, your mom really *is* the only one.

"One bottle, ready to go," I said, holding it up.

"Did you test it?" she asked.

What? Did she want me to drink some of it?

"Put a few drops on your wrist to make sure it's not too hot," she instructed me.

"Oh, right!" I said. *Duh.* Hadn't I seen this on TV a few times?

I tipped the bottle over, but instead of getting a few drops on my wrist, the whole top came off, and the milk poured all over my arm. I nearly screamed in pain. The liquid was *scalding*!

"Omigosh!" I said, then bit my lip.

Tears of pain stung my eyes, but I refused to let them spill over. I had almost burned out the inside of Lucas's mouth. How dumb was I?

"Oh! It's okay, Mary-Kate," Brittany's mom said. "You just forgot to tighten the top."

Apparently she was mistaking my pain for embarrassment over my mistake. Little did she know that not tightening the top of the bottle was the lesser of my mistakes.

I grabbed a towel from a clean pile on one of Lucas's shelves and quickly mopped up the mess. I didn't want Mrs. Bowen anywhere near it. If she noticed how hot the milk was, she would realize how incompetent I was and would never trust me around Lucas again.

"I'll go get another one," I said, gathering up the bottle and the soaked towel. "Back in a sec."

I rushed out and went to the bathroom. I stuck my hand under the faucet and turned on the cold water. The second it hit my skin, I sighed in relief. But pretty soon I found myself staring at my reflection in the mirror, looking into my own uncertain eyes.

How many things could I possibly get wrong? First the sleeping lesson, then the diapers, and now this! And how long was it going to be before Mr. and Mrs. Bowen found out how bad I was at this?

chapter eight

Thursday afternoon Brittany and I were studying in her room. Brittany was reading *Julius Caesar* for her English class, and I was studying up on World War II for a history quiz Mr. Thompson was giving us the next morning. The Bowens were out at work, and Lucas was taking his afternoon nap. It hadn't been this quiet in the house since I moved in.

"Ugh! Shakespeare's tragedies are so . . . tragic!" Brittany groaned, rolling over onto her back on the bed and dropping her book on the floor. "Seriously, I can't take it anymore. Why don't we get to read any of the comedies?"

"You think that's bad, try reading about Pearl Harbor," I replied, looking up. "This is seriously depressing."

There was a noise from the next room and Brittany and I looked at each other hopefully.

"Was that Lucas?" I asked.

"Maybe he's up from his nap," she said, sitting up straight. "If he's up from his nap, we should really go in there and play with him."

Lucas made another noise—a definitely awake noise—and we grinned. "Study break?" I said.

"Study break!" Brittany said as she jogged into the nursery.

"I'll go get his bear from the living room!" I said.

I pulled up the latch on the safety gate, raced downstairs, and grabbed the bear from the floor in front of the TV. On the way back up I took the steps two at a time. This was definitely one of the perks of having a baby around. It gave us a perfect excuse to get away from our books for a few minutes and clear our minds. When I went back to Pearl Harbor later, I was sure I would be refreshed and ready to absorb a lot more.

"Hey, Lucas! I have Mr. Brown!" I said, waggling the bear as I walked into the nursery.

Lucas and Brittany were sitting on the floor, and he reached out for the bear as I came in. He put the bear's head in his mouth for a second, then tossed it across the room. Brittany and I both laughed.

"Guess he wants to play with something else," I said.

"Let's raid the toy chest," Brittany suggested.

We opened the big box of toys at the back of the room and started to rummage through it.

"How about this?" I said, pulling out a plastic ring game. When I turned around to show it to Lucas, he was gone.

"Where did he go?" Brittany said.

My stomach clenched. "Oh no! The gate!"

Brittany's eyes widened, and we both ran for the hallway. Lucas was crawling at lightning speed right toward the stairs.

"Lucas!" Brittany shouted.

I made a dive for him and scooped him up off the carpet just as his hand started to go over the first step. Lucas giggled as I held him against my pounding heart.

"Phew! That was close," Brittany said, holding a hand over her own chest.

"Here! Take him!" I said, handing the baby to her. "Take him away from me! I cannot be trusted with your little brother."

My pulse was racing and I couldn't take it anymore. This was the last straw.

"Mary-Kate, what are you talking about? You

just forgot to put the gate back up," Brittany said. "It happens."

"I almost killed him!" I said, pacing back and forth in the hallway. "And it wasn't just this one time, okay? First I messed up his sleeping routine, and then . . . then I was mad because we missed *Newport Beach* to stop him from crying. And then, the other day, I ruined three diapers just trying to get one on him! And I forgot to test the bottle and almost gave the kid third-degree burns! I'm a walking disaster area!"

Brittany covered her mouth with her free hand and started to laugh.

"What? It's not funny!" I said.

"I'm sorry. You're right," Brittany said, still smiling. "But you're not a disaster area. Everything you just said? I did all of that, too, in the beginning."

"You did?" I asked, stopping in my tracks.

"Of course! All that and more!" Brittany said, walking back into the nursery and closing the door behind us. She placed Lucas on the floor, and he crawled right over to the ring game I had dropped when I ran out to save him. "Mary-Kate, come on. Did you think I was born with the knowledge of how to take care of a baby?"

I looked at her for a second. When she put it that way . . . it sounded pretty silly. "No. I guess not."

"It takes practice," she said. "You're not bad at this. You're just learning."

I felt my shoulders start to relax, and I dropped onto the love seat. "So I'm not a complete klutz-moron?" I asked with a smile.

"Not even," Brittany replied. She sat down next to me and draped an arm over my back as we watched Lucas play. "But will you at least admit that having a baby in the house isn't easy?"

"Oh, yeah. I'll admit that," I said with a relieved grin. "I'll admit that big-time."

"So you're having fun at Melanie's?" my mother asked me on the phone Thursday afternoon.

"Yeah, Mom. I'm having a great time," I said.

"Good. Well, tell her we said hello," my mother said. "I know you girls are enjoying your little adventures, but I'm looking forward to your coming home this weekend."

"We are, too, Mom. Really," I told her.

"Thanks, Ashley," she replied. "Love you!"

"Love you, too! Bye!"

I clicked off the phone and lay back in a lounge

chair by the pool in Melanie's backyard, trying to relax. It was a perfectly gorgeous day, just right for soaking up some rays and chilling with a friend. Unfortunately, even though I had told my mom that I was having fun, I couldn't seem to actually *chill*. Melanie and I hadn't said much to each other all day, and I was beginning to get a bit lonely.

It wasn't as if I hadn't tried, but Melanie was giving me nothing in return. Whenever I asked her a question, the answer was short and flat. I had a feeling she was still upset from the night before. I felt bad for her because I knew she was missing her dad, but I was also a little hurt because I really hadn't done anything wrong. The whole thing was making me very uncomfortable.

Then, out of nowhere, the sliding glass door behind us slid open, and out walked Mr. Han. "Hi, girls!"

"Dad! What are you doing here? It's only five o'clock," Melanie said, dropping her magazine and straightening up.

"Well, I realized how distracted I've been the past couple of days, so I decided to cut my work-day short," Mr. Han said, walking over and sitting down at the end of Melanie's chair. "Tonight we're all hanging out together."

Melanie hugged her dad and I was beyond relieved. Maybe now everything could go back to normal!

"Now, I'm going to be very busy for the next few days, so I have a proposal for you," Mr. Han said to Melanie. "How would you like to be one of my assistants at the fashion show?"

Melanie's mouth dropped open. "Are you kidding?" she asked.

"Absolutely not," he said with a pretend-serious face. "I never kid about my work."

"That would be so awesome!" Melanie cried, bouncing up and down on her chair. "Thanks, Dad!"

"Of course," he said, patting her knee. "And what about you, Ashley? Would you like to be an assistant as well?"

I almost jumped out of my skin. "No way! Really?"

"Yes way, really!" he replied, laughing.

"I would love to! Behind the scenes at a major fashion show? I mean, absolutely!" I said, just imagining the glamour and glitz of the weekend. "Thank you, Mr. Han."

"No, thank you!" he said. "It's going to be a lot of hard work. I hope you ladies are up for it."

"We totally are. Right, Mel?" I said, glancing at my friend for the first time.

My smile faltered a bit when I saw that her face had totally changed. She was no longer psyched. In fact, she looked a little disappointed. I couldn't understand why. Wasn't her father trying to make everything up to her? Wasn't this exactly what she wanted?

"Yeah. Sure we are," she said, forcing a smile.

"So, what do you two want to do for dinner tonight?" Mr. Han asked, standing up and rubbing his hands together.

"I noticed some ground turkey in the freezer," I said quickly, standing up. "I could make us some turkey burgers . . . you know . . . as a thank you."

Mr. Han smiled. "Sounds good to me. What do you think, Melanie? Can we let our houseguest cook for us?"

"Sure. Go crazy," Melanie said with a shrug.

I wasn't sure what had happened to make her fall flat again, but I couldn't ask. Not right there in front of her father.

"Well, I guess I'll go change out of my bathing suit and get cleaned up," I said, picking up my bottle of sunblock. "Why don't you guys hang out here? I'll call you if I need help."

"Yeah, Dad," Melanie said, brightening a little. "Tell me about your day."

"Sure. Thanks, Ashley," Mr. Han said, sitting down again.

As I went inside to shower, Melanie and her dad were chatting animatedly, and Melanie was all smiles once again. I just hoped that spending this time with her dad would knock her out of her funk. I wanted Melanie back to her old self. The old self that was my best friend.

"Wow! You're really going to be working backstage at the fashion show?" Mary-Kate asked.

"Yeah. How cool is that?" I said into the phone. I had taken it into one of the guest rooms so I could have a little privacy as I talked to my sister. Still, I knew that with the way sound carried in this house, Melanie and Mr. Han could probably hear everything I said.

"Ashley, that is so awesome," Mary-Kate said with a yawn.

"Are you okay?" I asked. "You sound tired."

"I am tired," Mary-Kate said. Then her voice dropped to a whisper. "Did I tell you that Lucas was up half the night again last night? Just when it seems like he's getting better about putting himself to sleep, he wakes up and starts crying again."

"Oh, no," I said, whispering as well. "No wonder you looked like you were going to pass out in English class."

"Did I?" Mary-Kate said. "Actually, come to think of it, I don't even remember what that class was about today."

"Well, maybe we should meet up after school tomorrow, and I'll give you my notes."

"I would, but Brittany and I promised to watch Lucas," Mary-Kate said. "The Bowens have their final meetings to go over plans for the fashion show."

"Oh," I said, feeling disappointed. "You know, I kind of can't wait until we're living together again."

"Tell me about it," Mary-Kate said with another yawn. "So what's up with Melanie's dad?"

I wanted to tell her, but I could hear Mr. Han walk in the house and answer his cell phone. If Melanie heard me talking about her, she might get even more upset than she already was.

"Not much. Everything's . . . fine," I said.

"Can't talk, huh?" Mary-Kate said.

"Not really," I replied. "Maybe tomorrow at school sometime. I should probably go."

"Me, too," Mary-Kate said. "The earlier I get to

bed, the more sleep time I get before Lucas wakes up."

"Good luck," I told her.

"You, too," she said.

After I hung up the phone, I went back to Melanie's room, and on the way I saw her father heading to his study. Melanie and I were alone on the second floor, so I decided it was about time we talked about whatever was bothering her.

"Melanie?" I said as she crawled into bed. "Did I do something wrong?"

"What? No!" she said, pulling her sheets up to her chin.

"Really? Because I kind of feel like you've been giving me the cold shoulder today," I said, getting into my bed.

Melanie took a deep breath and rolled over onto her side. She propped her head up on one hand and looked at me. "Okay, I know I'm going to sound like a big baby when I say this, but . . . I guess I'm kind of jealous," she said.

"Of what?" I asked.

"Of you."

"What? Why?" I asked.

"I don't know. I mean . . . my dad has never invited me to a dress rehearsal before, but then you're here, and he asks us both," she said. "And then when we were there, he took your suggestion about the outfit and not mine, and then he asked us *both* to be assistants at the show. Plus, do you know how many times I've offered to cook him a meal and been shot down? Look at what happened at breakfast the other day."

My heart squeezed a little bit tighter with each example she mentioned.

"It's almost like he likes you more than he likes me," she finished, picking at a piece of lint on the edge of her blanket.

"Melanie, you know that's not true," I said firmly. "Look, I'm sure your dad is just trying to be polite to me. I'm staying here this week, so he doesn't want me to feel left out or something."

Melanie sighed and rolled over onto her back. Something told me she didn't quite believe my logic.

"Whatever," she said, staring at the ceiling. "I guess I should just be happy that he was here all night tonight. I was starting to feel as if I was never going to get to hang out with him for more than an hour."

She reached over and turned out the light, plunging the whole room into darkness.

"Good night, Ashley," she said.

"'Night," I replied.

I lay down, an uncomfortable feeling of guilt and sorrow settling into my chest. I hoped Melanie wasn't mad at me. It sounded as if she knew I didn't really do anything wrong and that she was just upset with her father, but she still wasn't acting completely normal with me.

I sighed and stared into the darkness, thinking about my dad, my mom, and my sister. I was so happy that I had them and that I never had to doubt that they loved me and wanted to spend time with me. Until then I had never realized just how lucky I really was to have a family like mine.

chapter nine

"So, what are we going to wear to the fashion show tomorrow?" I asked Melanie as we walked up the front steps toward school the next morning.

"I think we have to wear all black like the other workers," she said. "One drawback of being an assistant," she added with a laugh. "No fabulousness allowed."

I smiled at her joke. It was the first one she had made in a couple of days. I figured it had to be a good sign.

"Oh, hey. There's Mary-Kate, Brittany, and Lauren!" Melanie said suddenly, then took off at a jog. I raced to catch up with her, clutching my books to my chest. Mary-Kate and the others paused as we approached.

"Hey! Where's the fire?" Mary-Kate asked.

"No fire. I just wanted to give you these," Melanie said, whipping a few tickets from the back pocket of her jeans.

Brittany took them, and Lauren's and Mary-Kate's eyes widened. "Second-row passes to your dad's fashion show?" Lauren exclaimed.

"Well, the press and the stars get front row," Melanie said with a shrug. "But these are almost as good."

"Omigosh! Melanie! This is totally incredible!" Mary-Kate said, hugging her. "You could have gotten us standing-room-only passes, and it still would have been incredible."

"I don't believe it," Brittany said. "With these tickets we can practically reach out and touch the models!"

"Yeah, but you probably shouldn't. I think they frown on that," Melanie joked.

"This is so cool," I said with a grin. "Now we all get to be there."

"Yes, but *you* are just the hired help," Mary-Kate joked, fanning herself with her ticket as she pretended to look down her nose at me. "We are the honored, second-row guests of the designer's daughter."

"Ha ha," I said, bumping her with my hip.

"I can't wait, Melanie. Thanks," Brittany said, pocketing her ticket.

"I'm glad I could do it," Melanie said. "It's really going to be a great show this year. This is the first time I've seen the designs beforehand, so it's the first time I can say that and really know what I'm talking about."

We all smiled, but I could tell there was a hint of sorrow behind Melanie's words. She was still upset with her father—still remembering that until this year she had been kept out of the loop.

"Well, see you guys in class," Melanie said. Then she turned and walked off toward her locker.

"What was that?" Lauren said once Melanie was out of earshot. "She seemed a little, I don't know, out of it."

"It's her dad," I said as we joined the crowd hustling down the hall. "Melanie says he's never around, and it really hurts her feelings. And the thing is, he doesn't really seem to notice. I think it's totally obvious that she's upset, but he's all smiles, as if everything's fine."

"Wow. What a mess," Brittany said. "Why doesn't she talk to him about it?"

"I think she doesn't want to upset him," I said. "She doesn't get to spend much time with him, so she wants it to be good time, not serious-talk time, you know?"

"I can sort of see that," Mary-Kate said.

"I don't know what to do, you guys," I told them, pausing by Brittany's locker. "I mean, she's really hurting, and I wish I could help."

"Why don't you talk to Mr. Han about it?" Mary-Kate suggested. "You can ask him to talk to Melanie."

"I thought about that, but I think I would be overstepping my bounds," I said. "I'm not his daughter, you know? Technically it's not really any of my business. Besides, Melanie might get mad."

"Sheesh. This really stinks," Lauren said. "I can't even imagine feeling like I couldn't talk to my dad."

"Me, neither," I said with a sigh.

"Don't worry about it," Mary-Kate told me, slipping an arm around my shoulders. "Just keep your eyes and ears open for the next couple of days. Who knows? Maybe you'll see an opportunity to help out."

"You do know people, Ashley. If anyone can do it, it's you," Brittany told me.

I smiled at their confidence and just hoped they were right. I couldn't take seeing Melanie this sad for much longer.

"Mom! Dad!" Brittany shouted as we walked into the house that afternoon. "You're never going to believe what Melanie got us!"

We rushed into the kitchen, where Mr. and Mrs. Bowen sat surrounded by papers, going over their plans for their next catering gig. Lucas was sitting in the high chair nearby, gnawing on a soft rattle.

"Wow! Must be something exciting!" Mrs. Bowen said.

"Don't keep us in suspense," Mr. Bowen put in.

Brittany and I whipped out our tickets and held them up, our grins wide. "Second-row tickets to her dad's show!" Brittany announced.

"How cool is that?" I put in, still giddy even though I had been looking at the ticket all day.

But Mr. and Mrs. Bowen didn't exactly jump onto the psyched-up bandwagon. Instead they exchanged a long look. A look that made me feel instantly doomed.

"What?" Brittany asked, her face falling. "What is it?"

"Well, your mother and I are working at Mr. Han's fashion show, remember?" Mr. Bowen said, setting a stack of papers aside.

"Oh . . . right," Brittany said.

"What?" I asked, not catching on.

"Well, we were hoping you girls could stay home and watch Lucas," Mrs. Bowen said. "We're going to be down at the beach most of the afternoon and evening."

"Oh," I said, my stomach turning.

"I'm sorry, girls," Mrs. Bowen said. "If I had known you were going to get tickets . . ."

"No. That's okay, Mrs. Bowen," I said, waving a hand. "Of course we'll stay with him. That's what big sisters are for, right?"

"Yeah," Brittany added. "It's not a problem."

"Thanks for being so great about this," Mr. Bowen said with a small smile.

"No problem," Brittany said. "We have a lot of homework to do, so . . ."

"It's Friday," her mother reminded us.

"Yeah, but you're always telling me not to put it off, right? Besides, you guys are leaving for that meeting soon, so we might as well do some while you're still watching the baby," Brittany said. "Come on, Mary-Kate. Let's go upstairs."

I followed her out of the kitchen. Over my shoulder I saw the Bowens look at each other again and wondered what they were thinking. Did they feel bad for us, or did they think we were being selfish by being disappointed?

"Well, I guess this is one of those sacrifices you're always talking about," I said as Brittany and I trudged up the stairs.

"I guess," she replied. "But this is the most major one I've ever had to make."

We looked down at our tickets, shrugged, and dumped them into her wastepaper basket as we walked into her bedroom.

"Bet you're wishing you'd gone to live with Melanie this week instead of me," Brittany said, dropping her bag and flopping onto her bed.

I flopped back from the other side so that our feet were on opposite sides of the bed, but our heads were right next to each other.

"Nah. I've had a lot of fun this week," I told her. "I think I'm just wishing that I could take Ashley's place tomorrow."

"Trust me," Brittany said with a sigh. "You're not the only one."

chapter ten

On Saturday morning I woke up to the sound of a car door slamming outside. Blinking the sleep from my eyes, I threw off the covers and glanced out the window to see Brittany's dad getting into his van and driving away. Downstairs I could hear the sounds of Mrs. Bowen cleaning up the kitchen. They were going to work separately today because they had so much to bring, they needed both their cars. Soon they were going to be serving their delicious food to all the fabulous fashionistas.

I sighed and glanced at the wastebasket where we had tossed our fashion show tickets. They looked so lonely and useless just sitting there.

"Hey," Brittany said, sitting up and stretching. "Ready for a fun-filled day with no models whatsoever?" she joked.

"You betcha," I replied.

I leaned over and pulled a pair of sweatpants and a T-shirt out of my open suitcase, which lay on the floor by a wall. I'd picked out the most killer outfit to wear to the fashion show, but I wasn't going to need it now. Old, grungy sweats were the order of the day.

"Girls! Are you awake? I made breakfast!" Brittany's mother called.

Brittany and I exchanged a smile and headed downstairs in our pajamas. Waiting on the kitchen table was a full pancake breakfast with coffee and freshly squeezed orange juice.

"You don't have to bribe us, Mom. We already said we'd babysit," Brittany joked.

"It's not a bribe," her mother said, running a hand over Brittany's hair. "I was up at five this morning thanks to my nerves, so I figured I might as well feed you girls."

"This is a really big job for you, huh?" I said as I poured myself a cup of coffee.

"Our biggest yet," Mrs. Bowen replied. "That's why it means so much to us that you girls are willing to help out."

"No problem," Brittany replied.

"It means so much to us, in fact, that we've

decided to let you off the hook," Mrs. Bowen said nonchalantly, taking a sip of her coffee.

Brittany dropped her fork with a clang, and our eyes met across the table. I could hardly let myself believe what I had just heard. Mrs. Bowen smirked over her coffee mug.

"You're letting us go?" Brittany said finally.

"Yep. Your father and I talked it over last night, and we decided to call a babysitter," Mrs. Bowen said.

"You're kidding!" I said, letting out a little squeal.

"You two have been so great this week, helping out with Lucas," Mrs. Bowen continued with a smile. "We both figured you deserved a break."

"You're kidding!" Brittany said, echoing me.

"Why does everyone think I'm kidding?" her mother said. "Don't I look serious?"

"Mom! You're the best!" Brittany said, jumping up from her seat and wrapping her arms around her mother.

I joined them in a big group hug. I couldn't help it. I felt as if I had just been given the coolest gift in the world.

"Thank you, thank you, thank you!" I said.

"You're welcome!" Mrs. Bowen replied as we

released her. "We called Carrie Bloom from down the street, and she should be here at noon. You girls can walk down to the show site, right? I need to take my car."

"Absolutely," Brittany said. "No problem."

"Great. Well, I should get going," her mother said, checking her watch. "Your father is probably already freaking out."

"Good luck, Mom!" Brittany said as her mom gathered her things.

"Yeah! Good luck!" I added.

"Thanks, girls. I'll see you there!" she called over her shoulder.

The second the door closed, Brittany and I jumped up and down, hugging each other and screaming. We were going to the fashion show after all!

The morning of the fashion show Melanie and I were brimming with excitement. We both put on plain black T-shirts, black pants, and black boots. I tied my hair back in a loose bun and applied some sensible yet sophisticated makeup. Melanie put her hair up with a pair of chopsticks, and we checked our reflections in her full-length mirror. Her eyes met mine and we grinned.

"We totally look the part," I said.

"Wardrobe assistants at Fashion Week," she replied. "We are so beyond cool."

"I know!"

I was so excited to see that Melanie was getting into the spirit of things. She had been so down in the dumps the past couple of days, I never knew what to expect from her. But even with everything that was going on in her life, she couldn't ignore the excitement of what we were about to do. In less than an hour we were going to be surrounded by models, photographers, fashion reporters, and probably even a few Hollywood stars!

"I can't wait to see what everyone is wearing," I said as we practically skipped downstairs.

"I know. I hope my dad gets good reviews," Melanie replied. "He's been working *so* hard."

"Where is he, anyway?" I asked.

"Probably in his office, obsessing," Melanie joked as I followed her into the kitchen for some breakfast.

"Good. I want to wish him luck," I told her.

"Me, too," she said with a smile.

We both paused as we entered the kitchen. There, in the center of the table, was a platter piled with bagels, a jug of coffee, and some spreads. Next to the food was a folded note.

"What's up?" I asked, as Melanie picked up the piece of paper.

She unfolded it, read it, and stopped smiling.

"He already left," she said, folding the note and sticking it into her front pocket. "He had to get there early to fix some last-minute staging issues."

"Oh, well. We'll see him there," I said.

"I didn't even get to wish him luck," Melanie said forlornly.

I reached out and squeezed her shoulder, wishing I knew what to say, wishing there was something I could do.

❀

"Wow. You look stunning," Brittany said when I walked into the nursery in my fashion show outfit. I was wearing my favorite low-slung jeans and a shimmery tank top with matching gold sandals.

"Thanks," I replied, grinning. "So do you."

Brittany had gone with a basic black dress. Very sophisticated.

"I still can't believe we're actually getting to go," I said, leaning over the side of the crib to smooth a hand over Lucas's soft hair. He was playing with a clear ring that had colorful beads inside it. He felt a little warm to the touch, but he was wearing footsie pajamas, and it was kind of warm in the house.

"I know," Brittany said. "At least we *will* get to go if Carrie ever shows up."

She checked her watch, and I looked at the Humpty Dumpty clock over the door. Carrie was already ten minutes late. If she didn't get here soon, we were going to be walking in after everyone else was seated. The last thing I wanted to do was look late and rude in front of all those important people.

Suddenly Lucas chucked his ring out of the crib and started to cry. At the exact same moment the phone rang. Brittany and I exchanged a look.

"You get the kid, I'll get the phone," she said. Then she raced out of the room as fast as she could in her strappy heels.

"Aw . . . come here, Lucas," I said, lifting him out of the crib. I bounced him up and down a little, which he normally liked, but he kept right on screaming.

"What's the matter?" I asked him in my cooing baby voice. "Is it your diaper? Are you hungry?"

Right then, as if in answer to my last question, Lucas opened his mouth and spit up all over my shoulder. It hit my skin and dribbled down the front of my top. I closed my eyes, and he continued to cry.

That did not just happen, I thought. *He did not just vomit on my perfect fashion show outfit.*

"Oh, no! Mary-Kate!" Brittany said, noticing the spit-up the second she walked into the room. "I'm so sorry!" She grabbed a cloth. "I should've warned you he does that sometimes. Mom says it usually doesn't mean anything. I'm just so used to it. . . ." She trailed off sadly as she tried to dab at the mess.

"It's okay," I said, handing the crying Lucas to her and trying to ignore the smell. "I'll just . . . go change into . . . something."

"Actually, that was Carrie on the phone," Brittany said, her face scrunched up as if she was afraid to say any more.

"She cancelled, didn't she?" I asked, my hands dropping down at my sides.

Brittany nodded. "She has some kind of family emergency," she said. "I didn't get the whole story. She had to go pretty quickly."

"I don't believe it," I said, visions of fabulous outfits and flashing lights flitting through my mind. "What are we gonna do?"

"You should go," Brittany said, barely audible

above Lucas's crying. "He's *my* little brother. There's no reason you should miss out."

I looked down at my outfit, at the stain on my top, and sighed. "No, you should go."

"Mary-Kate—"

"I'm serious," I said honestly. "Look at me. My outfit is already trashed. You still look awesome. You should just go."

"Are you sure?" Brittany asked.

"Yes, I'm sure," I said, taking Lucas back from her. He hiccupped and gulped, and his cries lessened to little sobs. "There will be other fashion shows."

I hope, I added silently.

"Well, alright," Brittany said. "But I'll have my cell phone if you need me. And remember, the fashion show is right down on the beach, so I can be home in no time if you want backup."

I laughed. "He's a baby, not a police stakeout," I said. "Go. Tell all the supermodels I said hi."

Brittany smiled a little sadly and gave me a half-hug on the nonspittle side of me.

"Thanks, Mary-Kate."

"No problem," I said. "Lucas and I will have fun. Once I calm him down." *And get myself cleaned up,* I thought.

"Okay. I'll see ya later!"

Brittany gave Lucas a kiss on the forehead, then headed out. I heard the back door close, and I sat down on the love seat with the baby. Lucas was still fussing a bit, and at that moment I felt like joining him.

Here I was, covered in baby spit-up, stuck inside for the rest of the day. Meanwhile Ashley was rubbing elbows with the coolest people in the fashion industry, meeting stars, and seeing all those incredible new clothes.

I bet she was having the time of her life.

chapter eleven

"Ashley! Ash! Have you seen any Vaseline anywhere?" Melanie asked me. She was completely breathless, and her hair was falling loose from her stylish bun. A line of sweat had appeared along her hairline. Not that I was surprised. I felt as if I had been running a marathon.

"Vaseline? Why would anyone need Vaseline?" I asked.

"I don't know! Something about her lipstick not getting onto her teeth," Melanie said, gesturing over her shoulder at one of the models.

Yuck, I thought. "Well, I guess if it was anywhere it would be with the other beauty supplies," I said, shifting the stack of tear sheets in my arms. Each sheet had a sketch of the original design, listed the exact components of each outfit, including accessories and makeup, and had a Polaroid clipped to it. I also had a roll of double-stick tape, a bottle of makeup remover, and a fistful of cotton balls in my grasp.

"Excuse me! You! Runner girl!" someone called out, snapping her fingers behind me.

I rolled my eyes. These people had been treating me like I was some kind of dog all day.

"Tried that," Melanie said as we both ignored the snapper. "It's not there."

"Well, try the other models," I suggested. "Maybe someone else is using it. Or maybe they brought their own."

"Got it," Melanie said and tore off.

"I *said*, excuse me," the snapper snapped.

I took a deep breath for patience and turned around. A tall woman in a black dress and tons of makeup hovered behind me.

"I need you to find me some nonaerosol hair spray," she said, waving a silver can of styling product at me. "I don't use anything that harms the environment."

"Sure. Okay," I said, whirling around and running right smack into Molly St. John's agent.

"Molly needs her own dressing room," she said flatly.

"Uh . . . sorry?" I said, still juggling all the stuff in my arms.

"Molly St. John does not dress in a communal dressing room like some run-of-the-mill model," the woman told me snidely. "It specifically states in her contract that she is to have her own dressing room, and I don't see it. Where is it?"

"I . . . well . . . I don't know," I said truthfully.

"You don't know," she repeated, looking down her nose at me. "What kind of people is Han hiring around here?"

"Excuse me! Can you get me some water, please?" someone called out.

"And I need safety pins over here, Ashley!" one of the dressers shouted.

"Where's that hair spray?" the finger snapper demanded.

I felt as if I was being pulled in a million directions. My pulse raced as I tried to figure out whom to answer first. Then, over the agent's shoulder, I saw Molly St. John waving her arms at me.

"*I don't care about the dressing room!*" she mouthed. Then she pointed at her agent and faked choking.

That was it. I couldn't help it. I cracked up laughing.

The agent's face instantly darkened. "Are you laughing at me?" she asked.

My heart dropped, but Molly came over to save the day. "Terese?" she said, wrapping her arms around the bony woman's shoulders. "May I see you for a second?"

Then she pulled the woman away and mouthed an apology over her shoulder.

I let out a sigh of relief. At least Molly St. John was human.

One outrageous request down, three more to go. I dumped my armload onto the nearest table, ran to the beauty supply room, and grabbed a can of nonaerosol hair spray. Then I snatched a bottle of water from the cooler by the food table and snagged some safety pins from the supply shelf by the bathroom. I clutched the items as I made my way back to the dressing area.

"Ashley!"

I jumped at the sound of my name shouted so loudly and dropped the safety pins. The little tin exploded all over the floor, scattering the pins everywhere. I closed my eyes and told myself there was no use in losing it. Losing it was not going to fix the situation. When I opened them again, Corinne, one of the dressers, was standing in front of me with a forlorn-looking model.

"Oops. Sorry," Corinne said, looking down at the mess.

"It's okay. What's up?" I asked her.

"Have you seen Mr. Han?" she asked.

"Not recently," I replied. "Why?"

"It's this outfit. It's just not working," she said, indicating the model and her tent-like brown dress. "I don't know what to do."

"What's the problem?" Melanie asked, appearing at my side.

"Zis dress is like a muumuu," the model said in a French accent. She held out her arms, and the neckline slipped right off her shoulders. "I think iz not supposed to be a muumuu."

"They must have sent the wrong size," Melanie said, biting her lip. "That can't be the design."

"Zis is what I said!" the model cried.

"So, what do I do? Do I pull her from the line-up? What?" Corinne asked.

"No. No. Then the timing will be all off," Melanie said. "Hang on. I think we can fix this. Just . . . don't move."

She ran off again. I smiled at the two women and went to hand out the hair spray and water. I noticed that the other dresser had found her own safety pins, so I made my way back to Melanie and Corinne. I paused at the end of a rack of clothing when I saw that Melanie was already hard at work on the outfit. She had found a brown, white, and black scarf and had cinched the dress around the model's waist. Now she was using tiny gold pins to fit the bodice to the girl's small frame. The model smiled, and Corinne looked impressed. Melanie was saving the day.

I heard Mr. Han talking and glanced up to see him chatting with a couple of people just outside the door. I heard Mary-Kate's voice in my head, telling me to keep an eye out for an opportunity to help. This was it. This was my chance.

"Excuse me, Mr. Han?" I said, stepping up to his side.

"Yes, Ashley?" he said as his companions hustled away with their instructions.

"There's something in here I think you should see," I told him.

Intrigued, Mr. Han followed me into the dressing room, and we both stood a few feet off to one side, watching Melanie work. She took a pin from between her teeth and finished off the fitting, then pulled a pair of hoop earrings from her pocket and handed them to the model. A few tugs on the skirt of the dress, and it fell perfectly into place. Melanie had just made an outfit out of what was basically a brown bag.

"Nice work, Mel," Corinne said.

Mr. Han took a step forward. "You did this?" he asked.

Melanie's face went slack, and she looked up at her dad. "Uh . . . yeah. They sent the wrong size, so I improvised. What do you think?"

"I think you have an incredible eye, Peaches," Mr. Han said, smiling proudly. "Not that I'm at all surprised."

Melanie beamed and I flushed with pleasure. I was so happy to see her so clearly psyched.

"In fact, I think your talents are being wasted as an assistant," Mr. Han said. "Why don't you stay with me in the wings and check the outfits before the models go on? I always need someone to help with last-minute accessories."

"Really?" Melanie asked with a gasp.

"Absolutely. Ashley seems to have everything under control back here," he said.

I *so* didn't, but I wasn't about to say anything. Melanie was getting everything she wanted.

"Are you sure you don't want Ashley instead?"

Melanie asked softly, glancing at me. "I mean, you did use her advice the other day at the dress rehearsal."

Mr. Han looked at me and smiled. "I did. And Ashley is clearly very stylish," he said. Then he turned back to Melanie. "But you're my trusted fashion authority, Peaches. You know that."

Melanie's grin widened. "Do you mind if I go, Ash?" she asked.

"Not at all," I told her.

She hugged me extra tightly, then walked off with her father. Suddenly I knew everything was going to be all right between Melanie and her dad. Even better, I knew that the discomfort between *me* and Melanie was gone. There was no way she could still be jealous of me after what had just happened. I couldn't have been happier.

"Um, hello? Runner girl?" someone said behind me. "Do you people have any breath mints around here?"

I felt my shoulders slump and turned around. As happy as I was, I realized that now I was going to have to deal with two dozen models and their agents and makeup artists all on my own. This was going to be interesting. . . .

"Come on, Lucas!" I whimpered, bouncing him up and down. "Tell me what's wrong. Tell Aunt Mary-Kate what's wrong."

As if he was really going to open his mouth and say his first words and they would make a full sentence. *Sure, Mary-Kate. Get a grip!*

But I couldn't help it. I was actually starting to lose my mind. Lucas had been crying for forty-five minutes straight, and I could not figure out why. Anyone would be losing it by this point.

"Hush, little baby, don't say a word. Mama's gonna buy you a mockingbird," I sang, swinging him back and forth.

My mother had sung that lullaby to me when I was a kid, and it always put me right to sleep. It was so soothing, so repetitive. But it did nothing for little Lucas. And, unfortunately, I only remembered the first few lines. It had always put me to sleep so fast, I never got to hear the end.

"Okay," I said, walking back and forth in the nursery and bouncing him on my hip. Lucas clutched my hair and pulled as he screamed, but I barely noticed. After a week of that I think my scalp was numb. "Okay, okay, okay. What next?"

I had already changed his diaper and tried to give him a bottle, but he had just batted it away.

He hadn't wanted any of his favorite toys either. Pretty soon I was going to have to call Brittany or her parents. There might be something really wrong with him. But I wasn't ready to do that just yet. I wanted to prove to them and to myself that I could take care of little Lucas. I racked my brain for an answer.

"Let's go downstairs," I whispered to Lucas, hugging him tightly.

He gulped and gasped and quieted down a little as I walked down the steps. Could this be all he wanted? To go downstairs? But the second I hit the living room floor, he started crying again. I sighed. I should have known it wouldn't be that easy.

I walked into the living room and felt something crush beneath my feet. It was the colorful box to Lucas's Snuggly Wugglies video. I nearly smacked my head at my own forgetfulness. Of course! Brittany had said the Snuggly Wugglies always worked, right?

I put Lucas down in his playpen and wheeled it over in front of the TV. The tape was still in the VCR from the other night, so I turned the TV on and hit PLAY. Instantly the Snuggly Wugglies appeared on the screen, and Lucas's eyes were riveted. For a long moment, he stopped crying.

"Oh, thank you! Thank you, whoever created these crazy tapes!" I said, collapsing onto the couch.

And then, five seconds later, Lucas started to scream again.

❀

"Have you seen Mark?" a harried-looking woman asked me.

"Mark?" I asked, trying not to drop any of the makeup compacts that were sliding around in my hands. "Who's Mark?"

"You don't even know who Mark is?" she asked.

"Um . . . no?" I replied. "There's Corinne," I said, lifting my chin. "She knows everyone. Why don't you ask her?"

The woman blew out a frustrated sigh but turned on her heel and stalked away. I whipped around and headed back toward the makeup station. I just had to get these pressed powders to Maria, the head makeup artist, and then I needed to find a pair of size nine black heels for one of the models. And there was something else. What was it . . . ?

"Ashley!"

Rasheem Martin, one of the show runners, jumped out of the supply closet and grabbed my arm. Every single one of the compacts slipped from my grasp. I tried to grab a few before they hit the ground, but I only ended up knocking them farther away. One of them ricocheted off a wall and skidded across the floor, where a hairstylist promptly stepped on it and hit the deck. I closed my eyes and winced. This was not good.

Rasheem didn't even seem to notice. "Come here. I need you," he said, dragging me into the supply closet.

"What is it?" I asked.

"Jessica needs double-stick tape, and I can't find any," Rasheem said, panicking. "Where is it?"

I turned around, plucked a roll off tape of the shelf, and handed it to him. Rasheem looked at me, all apologetic.

"Oh. It was right there, huh? Sorry. I kind of forgot to wear my glasses," he said.

"No problem," I replied.

I can do this, I thought. Then, taking a deep breath, I went out to gather the fallen makeup. Once I had retrieved all the compacts and chucked the broken ones, I delivered them to Maria. I was about to escape the makeup area when one of the models grabbed my arm.

"I need some water," she said. "As soon as possible."

"Water. Check," I said with a nod. At least I knew exactly where that was.

I headed out into the hallway and over to the table where all the snacks were displayed. The cooler, however, was gone. I crouched on the floor to check under the table, but it wasn't there. The bottled water had disappeared.

"Rasheem!" I shouted, grabbing him as he raced by. "Where did the water go?"

He looked at the spot on the floor where the cooler had been and squinted. "I don't know," he said before rushing away.

I looked around helplessly. "Corinne! Did you see anyone take a cooler out of here?" I shouted.

She shook her head and continued with her work. I asked another half dozen people, but no one had an answer, and everyone was too busy to help me look. Someone had made off with all our drinks!

Finally, at a loss for what else to do, I grabbed a paper cup from the table and jogged into the bathroom. I ran the tap until the water was ice-cold and filled the cup. Balancing it carefully and hoping no one else would jump out of a closet and surprise me, I brought the cup of water back to the model.

"Here you go!" I said with a smile, placing the cup on the makeup counter in front of her.

She looked at it as if it was filled with pickle juice. Her nose scrunched up, and her mouth curled into a sneer. "Is that from the tap?" she asked, pulling her hand away as if the cup might bite her.

"Yeah. We kind of have a shortage of the bottled water," I told her with my best innocent smile.

"No bottled water?" another model said, overhearing. "You must be joking."

"I can't do a show if there's nothing for me to drink," a third model whined. "This is ridiculous."

"I'm parched," another young woman said, opening her mouth like a fish. "I need water now."

The model who had originally asked for the water—no, *demanded* the water—eyed me with a self-satisfied smirk. I couldn't believe it. She was *happy* she had caused a scene. It was as if these people *lived* for drama! And now I was the villain of that drama.

I need to put these people in their place, I thought, looking around. But how could I? There were over twenty of them! And they were all angry and famous and . . . bigger than me!

My pulse pounded in my ears. My face heated up. I was no good at confrontation. No good at all.

Luckily, I happened to know someone who was. . . .

111

chapter twelve

Lucas was still crying. It had been far too long. I was shocked he hadn't exhausted himself to sleep by now. I was exhausted just *looking* at him. Finally I knew what I had to do. It was time to admit defeat and call Brittany.

"Okay, Lucas. I'm gonna get your sister now," I whispered into his ear. He was sitting on my lap, but he was crying so loudly, I was sure he couldn't hear me. I was more saying it for myself. I needed calming, too, at this point. "Or maybe even your mom!" I added. "You wanna see your mom, right? That's what this is all about?"

I stretched to the table at the end of the couch and grabbed the cordless phone. The second it was in my hand, it rang. I was so startled, I almost dropped it.

"Oh please, please, *please* let this be one of the Bowens," I said. I hit the TALK button and brought the phone to my ear. "Hello?"

"Mary-Kate! It's me, Ashley."

"Thank goodness! Ashley, you have to help me," I blurted, bouncing Lucas up and down in my lap.

"No! *You* have to help *me*!" she cried.

"Why? What's wrong?" I asked.

"Wait a minute. Is that *Lucas*?" Ashley said. "Is he okay? Did he hurt himself? Mary-Kate, you have to watch him every single second."

"I have been! I swear!" I replied. "He just will not stop crying no matter what I do." I stood up and walked around with Lucas in one arm and the phone pressed to my ear. "So? What do you need help with?"

"A couple dozen evil models," Ashley whispered. "Melanie's dad took her off to help him backstage, and she left me alone with them."

"Oh. What are they doing?" I asked, confused. It wasn't as if she was sitting a bunch of babies or something. These were adults we were talking about.

"They're about to go crazy on me, Mary-Kate," she whispered. "I lost the water cooler somehow, and they're staging a revolt. If I don't find them something other than tap water soon, you're gonna be an only child."

"They can't be that bad," I said over Lucas's crying.

"Worse," Ashley replied. "They all have long fingernails. *Manicured* ones. And I don't think they're afraid to use them. You have to get down here and help me."

"But what about the baby?" I asked, looking at Lucas's wet face.

"Bring him here with you," Ashley suggested. "Maybe I can figure out what's wrong with him. You know I'm good with babies."

"I don't know if the Bowens would like that," I said.

"So call them. I'm sure they wouldn't like the idea of their kid crying off the wall while you feel helpless," Ashley told me. "I don't think they'd want either of you to be this miserable."

"Good point," I said. "Okay. I'll be there as soon as I can."

"Thanks, Mary-Kate," Ashley said. "And hurry."

I hung up the phone and quickly dialed the Bowens' cell phone. It rang and rang until the voice mail picked up. I figured they must be somewhere really noisy and couldn't hear it. I tried

Brittany's number next. It picked up right away and went to voice mail. I let out a little groan of frustration while I listened to Brittany's chipper message.

"Brit, it's me," I said at the beep. "Listen, if you get this, find your parents and ask them to send a few dozen bottles of water back to the dressing rooms. Ashley needs them. And I hope you guys don't mind, but I have to bring Lucas down there. I left a message for your parents, but he's miserable and I don't know what else to do. Okay . . . see you in a few. Bye!"

I turned off the phone and dropped it onto the couch. I was about to put Lucas into his stroller when I remembered we were going to have to walk on the beach to get to the fashion show tents. A stroller would never work in the sand. I went to the front closet and pulled out the contraption I had seen Mr. Bowen carry the baby in. The straps went over his shoulders like a backpack, but the pack part, where the baby would be held, was in the front, so the baby was against his chest. I put Lucas down in his playpen and secured the carrier to me.

"Okay, Lucas. We're going for a little walk," I told him, lifting him up again. I placed him in the carrier and strapped him in. He was still crying, waving his little fists around.

"Don't worry," I told him as I grabbed his diaper bag and headed out the back door toward the beach. "Ashley will know what to do."

And if she doesn't, we'll find your parents, I thought. *I just hope they don't mind our crashing the show.*

The dressing room at the fashion show had become mass confusion. All the models were up in my face, shouting different demands and questions. A girl in a dark blue wig kept clucking her tongue and looking around her as if she just could not believe how incompetent I was.

"I don't understand," she said, throwing her arms up. "How can you be out of water?"

"We're not *out* of water," I said, desperate for them to listen, which none of them seemed to be doing. "We just misplaced it."

"How do you *misplace* water? It should be everywhere," one of the models said.

"We need water," another girl said. "We're *performers*. We need to stay hydrated."

"Well, I've looked everywhere for it. What do you want me to do?" I asked, at the end of my rope.

"We want you to do your job," Blue Wig said, her eyes flashing.

"Find your boss. Or . . . or go to the store," one of the other models demanded. "This is ridiculous. Telling the assistants how to do their jobs was not in my contract!"

At this last remark angry tears sprang to my eyes. They were insulting me right to my face! How could anyone act this way? They were models! They were supposed to be some of the coolest people on the planet. It turned out they were just a bunch of selfish, whiny babies.

I had to get out of there. Forget this crazy job. I had to go.

But Melanie and her father were counting on me! What could I do?

"Alright, people! Back away from the sister!"

Mary-Kate! Her voice was like music to my tortured ears.

I turned around to see her marching into the room. Lucas was in a baby carrier on her chest. I had never been so happy to see anyone in my life, but behind her was an even more welcome sight. Ten members of the Bowens' wait staff walked in, each carrying ice buckets full of bottled water. The models forgot all about me and descended on the wait staff like a bunch of hikers who had been lost for days in the desert.

I leaned back against the makeup counter. Suddenly I could breathe again.

"Thank you *so* much," I said to Mary-Kate.

"No problem. Here. Take Lucas. Maybe you can figure out what's wrong," Mary-Kate told me. She extracted Lucas from his carrier and handed him over to me.

The poor kid looked miserable. He had tears in his eyes and on his face, and he kept trying to shove one fist into his mouth.

"Mary-Kate, is he teething?" I asked.

"I don't know. Why?" Mary-Kate asked.

"I need his bag," I told her.

"Work your magic," she said.

She gave me the diaper bag and turned to the crowd of models. Suddenly there was a sharp whistle, and everyone shut up. Twenty-four beautiful faces turned to look at Mary-Kate, who stepped up onto a chair to address them. I grinned as I dug through the diaper bag. Thank goodness she was here.

"Alright, you have water," Mary-Kate said. "The show starts in ten minutes. Whatever you need, we will take your requests in an orderly fashion."

Every one of them clamored in Mary-Kate's direction, elbowing each other out of the way to get to her first. Once again it was total chaos.

"Hey! I said *orderly*!" Mary-Kate shouted, raising her hands in front of her.

The models stopped again and exchanged impressed glances. Suddenly they were lining up in a single-file line, looking up at Mary-Kate expectantly. This was the greatest thing I had ever seen!

"Aha! Found it!" I said, pulling a little blue teething ring and a bottle of children's pain reliever out of the bottom of the bag.

I handed the ring to Lucas, and he shoved it into his mouth and started to gnaw. The tears stopped flowing, and he gave me half a smile. When he gurgled, Mary-Kate looked down at us, and her jaw dropped.

"Hang on a sec," she told Blue Wig as she jumped down from her perch.

"You are a miracle worker! What did you do?" Mary-Kate asked me, bending at the waist to smile at little Lucas.

"He's got a tooth coming in," I told her. "It helps them if they have something to chew on."

"How did you know?" Mary-Kate asked me.

"He was trying to bite off his own hand, Mary-Kate," I said. "You didn't notice?"

"I thought he was just upset," she told me. She took a deep breath and sighed.

I knew how relieved she must feel. Sitting with a crying baby and not knowing what to do was just as frustrating and scary as facing down a couple dozen unreasonable models.

"Should we give him that?" she asked, gesturing at the pain reliever.

"We should ask his parents first," I replied. "But he's okay for now."

"Wow. I am totally impressed," Mary-Kate said.

"So am I," I said, glancing over my shoulder at the line of models.

Mary-Kate reached out and slapped my free hand. Clearly, if we were going to try out new families, we should have stuck together. In our lives, it was all about teamwork.

chapter thirteen

Working together, it didn't take me and Ashley very long to get everything under control. We restocked the supplies in the makeup room. We helped some of the models stuff shoes that were too big so that they wouldn't slip on the runway. We even gave our opinion on a wig for Molly St. John. How cool is that?

Brittany joined us backstage, and she was sitting in a makeup chair, holding little Lucas, while all the models bent around him, cooing and tickling him. The show was about to start, and Ashley and I actually had a chance to take a breather. We sat down in a couple of armchairs and watched Lucas and his fan club from across the room.

"Would you look at him?" Ashley said. "He is just so cute. Everyone loves him."

"I know. The models are all over him. Imagine how jealous the guys at school would be right now," I said with a smirk.

Ashley snorted a laugh. "Seriously."

Mrs. Bowen walked into the room in her serving tuxedo and looked around, her brow wrinkled in concern. I stood up the second I saw her, and when she spotted me, she raced right over.

"Mary-Kate? Is everything all right?" she asked me. "Where's Lucas?"

"He's right here, Mom," Brittany said.

"Thirty seconds to curtain!" the stage manager hissed, sticking his head into the room. "Let's go, girls!"

All the models groaned at the thought of being torn away from little Lucas. They planted a bunch of kisses on his forehead, then scurried from the room. Mrs. Bowen walked over and took Lucas from Brittany's arms. She felt his head, gave him a kiss, and hugged him.

"I'm really sorry about bringing him down here," I said, pushing my hands into the back pockets of my jeans. "He just wouldn't stop crying, and I didn't know what else to do."

"Well, you did the right thing," Mrs. Bowen replied. "I understand how confusing it can be. It's too bad babies can't simply tell us what's wrong."

"That would make life a lot easier," I agreed with a smile.

"I'm sorry about the babysitter," Mrs. Bowen said, sitting down and rubbing Lucas's back. "I really wanted you girls to be able to enjoy yourselves today."

"Don't worry about it," I said, raising a hand. "I signed on to be a big sister this week. I was just doing my job."

Mrs. Bowen smiled. "Well, you're officially relieved of duty," she said. "I'm going to take Lucas for a little while so that you girls can watch the fashion show."

"Mom, that's okay," Brittany said. "We can—"

"No! I insist," her mother said, gathering up the diaper bag. "As long as you take him afterward so that I can work the party. Do we have a deal?" she asked, looking from me to Brittany and back again.

"Deal," we both said, grinning.

Outside on the stage the music started up, a dance beat pounding so hard that the light fixtures over our heads started to shake. A cheer went up from the audience and we knew the show was starting. I got butterflies in my stomach just thinking about it. The excitement in the air was contagious.

"Okay, go. Have fun!" Mrs. Bowen said. "I'll see you in a little while."

"Bye, Lucas!" we all called out, waving at him as he looked at us over his mom's shoulder. He giggled and buried his face in his mother's hair.

"Come on! Let's go find Melanie and her dad!" Ashley said, grabbing my hand.

I followed her, but I couldn't help glancing behind me for one last look at Lucas. Maybe I really was becoming a big sister. I missed the little cutie already.

❀

"Hey!" I whispered to Melanie, sneaking up behind her as she stood in the wings with her dad.

"Hi!" she replied with a glowing grin. She flashed a confused look when she saw that Brittany and Mary-Kate were with me, but she gave us all a big hug. "Where's Lauren?"

I peeked out at the audience and saw Lauren in her second-row seat, next to two empty chairs. She probably would have been wondering where Mary-Kate and Brittany were if she wasn't so entranced by the clothes.

"She's taking it all in," I said.

124

"Oh, good. So, how cool is this?" she asked.

"So totally cool," Mary-Kate said, stepping up next to her.

The four of us gathered together in a tight little knot, bursting with excitement as we watched each of the models strut out onto the stage, do a little turn, and then make her way down the catwalk. They all looked so beautiful and regal out there. I could hardly believe that these same people had been whining at me about tap water twenty minutes ago.

Each outfit was more gorgeous than the last. The reporters and buyers and critics in the audience were riveted. Flashbulbs popped from every corner of the room, sending purple dots dancing across my vision. I laughed at the spectacle of it all, but also because I couldn't believe we were actually here. We had pulled it off and we were witnessing the launch of a brand-new line of clothes. After all the hard work, the yelling, and the confusion, it really was like a dream come true.

"Mr. Han, the clothes are so incredible," Brittany said.

"Thank you, Brittany," he said. "That means a lot coming from you. I consider you girls to be my most important critics."

Brittany beamed, and Melanie grabbed my hand. "Oh! Look at that one! That scarf and the brooch in her hair were my ideas!" she said with a happy giggle.

"Wow. That's so cool," I replied, squeezing her fingers. "Very dramatic."

"You think that's good? She pulled this next outfit together all on her own," Mr. Han said with a proud smile as Molly St. John walked out onto the stage. She was wearing a sleek, low-cut gown. From her ears hung the longest crystal earrings I had ever seen. They perfectly matched the silver crystal sandals that peeked out from the hem of the gown as she walked. When she turned around, I saw that the bun in her hair was draped with a string of crystals woven into her hair and cascading down her back.

"I turned a necklace into a hairpiece," Melanie told me. "I just thought it worked."

The audience let out a murmur of surprise when they saw Molly's back view. A couple of reporters scribbled crazily in their notebooks. Melanie grinned.

"Apparently you were right," Mary-Kate said. "They love it!"

"She's always right," Mr. Han said, putting an

arm around Melanie's shoulders and giving her a hug. "I don't know why I didn't realize it sooner."

Melanie cuddled into her dad's side and closed her eyes, perfectly content. And why not? She had accessorized Molly St. John. The audience loved her work. Most important, her dad loved her work, and he clearly loved her. Everything had worked out the way it should.

Before we knew it, it was over. All the models lined up on the catwalk, and Melanie's dad was announced. He leaned down and gave Melanie a quick kiss on the forehead.

"You did great, Dad," she said.

"Thanks, Peaches," he replied. "I think *we* did great."

Then he grabbed her hand and pulled her out onto the stage to take his bow with him. The crowd went crazy, jumping to their feet. Lauren shouted louder than everyone else. Melanie and Mr. Han walked all the way to the end of the cat- walk, the models applauding them and kissing them as they went. At the very end of the stage Mr. Han raised Melanie's hand in the air, and together they made a triumphant bow.

"The whole place is going crazy," Mary-Kate said. "This is so incredible."

"Yeah," I replied, though I didn't really notice any of the commotion. I was too busy staring at my friend—at the happiest smile I had ever seen.

❋

"Melanie, your dad is, like, a superstar," I said, watching as dozens of reporters jostled for a few words with Mr. Han.

"I know!" she said, taking a sip of her sparkling cider. "I overheard one of the critics say this was my dad's best show yet."

"I completely agree," Lauren said. "Not that I've seen any of the other ones."

We laughed, and Brittany grabbed Lucas's hand as he reached for a champagne flute. We were all sitting at a table at the reception following the show, watching as the rich and famous mingled around us. Every once in a while someone would stop at our table to either congratulate Melanie or gush over baby Lucas. It was as if we had our own celebrities at our table.

"We really should feed him," Brittany said as Lucas started to fuss. "Mary-Kate, can you grab some food?"

"I'm on it," I said, reaching for the diaper bag.

"I still can't believe you brought him here," Melanie said as I retrieved a little jar of pureed carrots. "I mean, a baby at a fashion show?"

"Hey, my sister needed me," I replied.

"Wait a minute. You needed me as much as I needed you," Ashley put in.

I popped the top on the jar of food and handed it to Brittany with a little plastic spoon from Lucas's bag.

"This is true," I said. "I mean, look at the kid. He's a total terror."

Brittany fed him a spoonful of carrots, and Lucas swallowed, then laughed, shaking his arms up and down in delight.

"Yeah. Scare-*ry*," Lauren said sarcastically.

We all laughed as Lucas giggled and reached out toward the jar of food again.

"So," Brittany said, scooping up another serving of carrots. "What have we learned this week?"

She and Melanie looked at us with sly expressions. Melanie leaned back in her chair and raised one eyebrow as she waited for an answer.

"Hmmm . . . let's see," I said, bringing a finger to my chin as if I was thinking it over. "We've learned that . . . your lives completely stink?" I said innocently.

Ashley cracked up, and Melanie and Brittany rolled their eyes.

"Ha ha. Very funny," Brittany said. "Our lives do not stink, right, Melanie?"

"Right," Melanie replied with a nod.

Just then Lucas spit out a mouthful of carrots, splattering Brittany's dress and dotting her face with orange droplets. Lucas giggled as if he thought it was the funniest thing in the world. Brittany's shoulders slumped, and I laughed, tossing her a towel from Lucas's bag.

"You were saying?" Ashley joked.

"See? I told you it was a piece of cake!" Brittany said, mopping herself up.

"I think we learned we were better off where we were. Stained dresses and all," Ashley said.

My heart warmed and I smiled, knowing that the ketchup-dress debacle was finally, truly and completely forgotten.

"Exactly," I said.

I looked at Lauren, Brittany, Melanie, and Lucas. It had been an interesting week, but I knew now more than ever that we all had to live our own lives. I couldn't wait to get back to my house and my bedroom and to having Ashley right across the hall.

"We love you guys," I said with a grin. "But it's definitely time for me and Ashley to go home."

Win A $500 Shopping Spree

One Grand-Prize Winner

will enjoy a day of shopping!

Mary-Kate and Ashley

Mary-Kate and Ashley Sweet 16
$500 Shopping Spree Sweepstakes

OFFICIAL RULES:

1. **No purchase or payment necessary to enter or win.**

2. **How to Enter.** To enter, complete the official entry form or hand print your name, address, age, and phone number along with the words *"Sweet 16* Win A Shopping Spree Sweepstakes" on a 3" x 5" card and mail to: *"Sweet 16* Win A Shopping Spree Sweepstakes" c/o HarperEntertainment, Attn: Children's Marketing Department, 10 East 53rd Street, New York, NY 10022. Entries must be received no later than June 28, 2005. Enter as often as you wish, but each entry must be mailed separately. One entry per envelope. Partially completed, illegible, or mechanically reproduced entries will not be accepted. Sponsor is not responsible for lost, late, mutilated, illegible, stolen, postage due, incomplete, or misdirected entries. All entries become the property of Dualstar Entertainment Group, LLC and will not be returned.

3. **Eligibility.** Sweepstakes open to all legal residents of the United States (excluding Colorado and Rhode Island), who are between the ages of five and fifteen on June 28, 2005 excluding employees and immediate family members of HarperCollins Publishers, Inc., ("HarperCollins"), Parachute Properties and Parachute Press, Inc., and their respective subsidiaries and affiliates, officers, directors, shareholders, employees, agents, attorneys, and other representatives and their immediate families (individually and collectively, "Parachute"), Dualstar Entertainment Group, LLC, and its subsidiaries and affiliates, officers, directors, shareholders, employees, agents, attorneys, and other representatives and their immediate families (individually and collectively, "Dualstar"), and their respective parent companies, affiliates, subsidiaries, advertising, promotion and fulfillment agencies, and the persons with whom each of the above are domiciled. All applicable federal, state and local laws and regulations apply. Offer void where prohibited or restricted by law.

4. **Odds of Winning.** Odds of winning depend on the total number of entries received. Approximately 300,000 sweepstakes announcements published. Prize will be awarded. Winner will be randomly drawn on or about July 15, 2005, by HarperCollins, whose decision is final. Potential winner will be notified by mail and will be required to sign and return an affidavit of eligibility and release of liability within 14 days of notification. Prize won by a minor will be awarded to parent or legal guardian who must sign and return all required legal documents. By acceptance of the prize, winner consents to the use of their name, photograph, likeness, and biographical information by HarperCollins, Parachute, Dualstar, and for publicity purposes without further compensation except where prohibited.

5. **Grand Prize.** One Grand Prize Winner will receive a $500 cash prize to be used at winner's discretion.

6. **Prize Limitations.** Prize will be awarded. Prize is non-transferable and cannot be sold or redeemed for cash. No cash substitute is available. Any federal, state, or local taxes are the responsibility of the winner. Sponsor may substitute prize of equal or greater value, if necessary, due to availability.

7. **Additional terms:** By participating, entrants agree a) to the official rules and decisions of the judges, which will be final in all respects; and to waive any claim to ambiguity of the official rules and b) to release, discharge, and hold harmless HarperCollins, Parachute, Dualstar, and their respective parent companies, affiliates, subsidiaries, employees and representatives and advertising, promotion and fulfillment agencies from and against any and all liability or damages associated with acceptance, use, or misuse of any prize received or participation in any Sweepstakes-related activity or participation in this Sweepstakes.

8. **Dispute Resolution.** Any dispute arising from this Sweepstakes will be determined according to the laws of the State of New York, without reference to its conflict of law principles, and the entrants consent to the personal jurisdiction of the State and Federal courts located in New York County and agree that such courts have exclusive jurisdiction over all such disputes.

9. **Winner Information.** To obtain the name of the winner, please send your request and a self-addressed stamped envelope (residents of Vermont may omit return postage) to *"Sweet 16* Win A Shopping Spree Sweepstakes" Winner, c/o HarperEntertainment, 10 East 53rd Street, New York, NY 10022 after August 15, 2005, but no later than February 15, 2006.

10. **Sweepstakes Sponsor:** HarperCollins Publishers.

Mary-Kate and Ashley Sweet 16

BOOK SERIES

New York Times bestselling series

For Mary-Kate and Ashley, their sweet sixteenth birthday was the ultimate party, a memory to last a lifetime. But it was just the beginning of the greatest year of their lives. Because anything can happen when you're sweet sixteen . . .

Don't miss the other books in the Sweet 16 book series!

- ❏ Never Been Kissed
- ❏ Wishes and Dreams
- ❏ The Perfect Summer
- ❏ Getting There
- ❏ Starring You and Me
- ❏ My Best Friend's Boyfriend
- ❏ Playing Games
- ❏ Cross Our Hearts
- ❏ All That Glitters
- ❏ Keeping Secrets

- ❏ Little White Lies
- ❏ Dream Holiday
- ❏ Love and Kisses
- ❏ Spring into Style
- ❏ California Dreams
- ❏ Truth or Dare
- ❏ Forget Me Not

It's What YOU Read.

BOOK SERIES

Mary-Kate and Ashley are off to White Oak Academy, an all-girl boarding school in New Hampshire! With new roommates, fun classes, and a boys' school just down the road, there's excitement around every corner!

Coming soon wherever books are sold!

Don't miss the other books in the TWO of a kind book series!

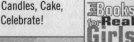